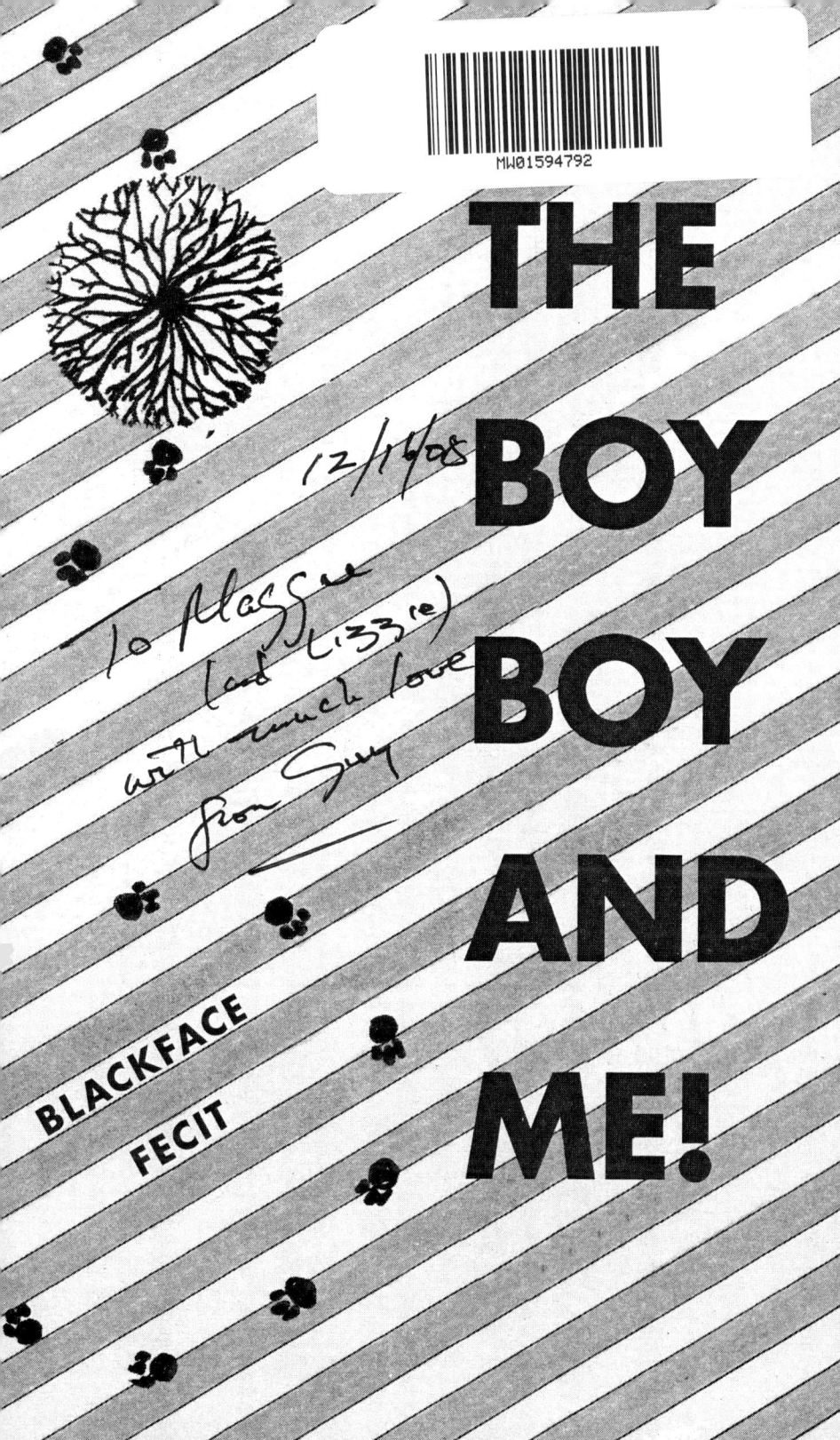

MW01594792

THE BOY BOY AND ME!

12/16/08

To Maggie
(and Lizzie)
with much love
from Guy

BLACKFACE
FECIT

As told to and transcribed by Eldon LaCroix
Edited by Eason Cross, Jr.
Polished by Guy Philbin

Order this book online at www.trafford.com/07-2920
or email orders@trafford.com

Most Trafford titles are also available at major online book retailers.

Note for Librarians: A cataloguing record for this book is available from Library and Archives Canada at www.collectionscanada.ca/amicus/index-e.html

Printed in Victoria, BC, Canada.

ISBN: 978-1-4251-6363-1

We at Trafford believe that it is the responsibility of us all, as both individuals and corporations, to make choices that are environmentally and socially sound. You, in turn, are supporting this responsible conduct each time you purchase a Trafford book, or make use of our publishing services. To find out how you are helping, please visit www.trafford.com/responsiblepublishing.html

Our mission is to efficiently provide the world's finest, most comprehensive book publishing service, enabling every author to experience success. To find out how to publish your book, your way, and have it available worldwide, visit us online at www.trafford.com/10510

www.trafford.com

North America & international
toll-free: 1 888 232 4444 (USA & Canada)
phone: 250 383 6864 ♦ fax: 250 383 6804
email: info@trafford.com

The United Kingdom & Europe
phone: +44 (0)1865 722 113 ♦ local rate: 0845 230 9601
facsimile: +44 (0)1865 722 868 ♦ email: info.uk@trafford.com

10 9 8 7 6 5 4 3 2

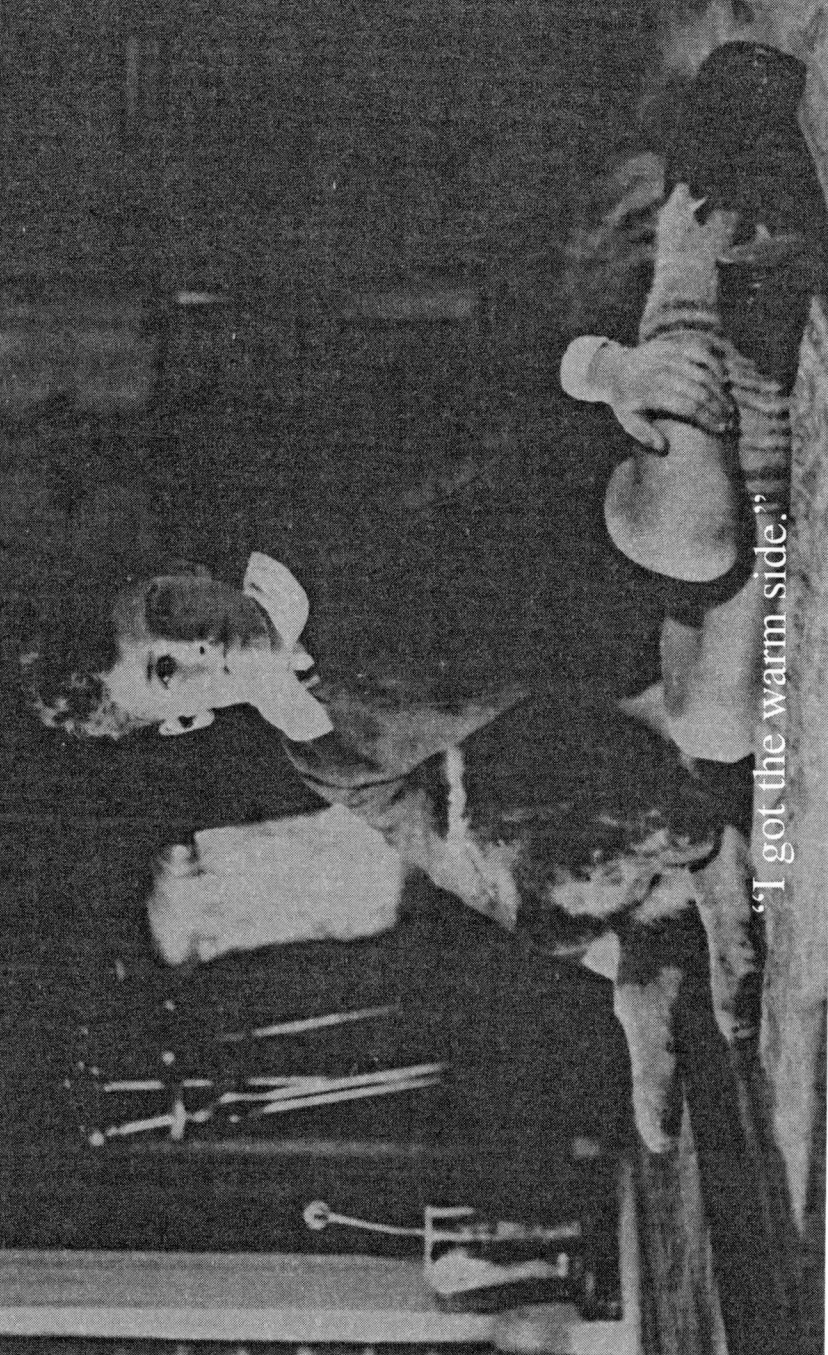

"I got the warm side."

THE BOY BOY AND ME!

By "Blackface"
as told to Eldon LaCroix

Edited by Eason Cross, Jr.

POOH CORNER PRESS
ALEXANDRIA, VIRGINIA
© 2008 ALL RIGHTS RESERVED

TABLE OF CONTENTS

Dedicated to
those mentioned who unwittingly
became key elements in the editor's life.
To
Diana Linnea Rosemond Johnson Cross
my wife of 57 years
mother to four excellent people:
Bennett Eason
Rebecca Hardwick
Amy Willard
Susan Mallette
It was written for
Alexander and Cooper Mackenzie
and
Will and Georgia Bermingham

Some of My Favorite Quotations:

Pooh Bah, in the "Mikado"
"Merely corroborative detail intended to give artistic verisimilitude to an otherwise bald and unconvincing narrative."
— W.S. Gilbert

King John, from "Now We Are Six"
"And, Oh, Father Christmas, if you love me at all,
Bring me a big red India-rubber ball."
— A.A. Milne

A Child's Geography of the World, 1929
"Just suppose you could go way, way off in the sky, sit on a corner of nothing at all, and look down at the World through a spyglass."
— V.M. Hillyer

The Old Hound, in the "Mischievous Dog" Fable
"That to be famous is not to be admired"
— Aesop

"Good Dog!"
— Rev. LaCroix

The Boy Boy and Me!

by "Blackface"

CHAPTER ONE: THE LACROIX
IN WHICH BLACKFACE GETS
AN ELEMENTARY EDUCATION

Animal Rescue

On hearing the doorbell jangle, I looked up to see this odd-looking gentleman entering the Animal Rescue League kennel in Boston. I instantly liked the peaceful look on his face, so rare on people, who are all so stern when not in animate conversation. His odd look came from the plain black suit he was wearing, the peculiar gray bib on his chest, and his collar on backwards.

He greeted my keeper cordially with "A good day to you, Sir," and "I see you have many splendid dogs here this afternoon." I took this personally as a compliment and would have gone up and licked his hand had I been free to do so. The man then told my keeper in a strong and friendly voice that he was looking for the kind of dog that could be a companion for his little boy, soon to be five years old.

Now, I must interject at this point in my tale to tell you that I am a most precocious canine. I can understand human speech. I can follow thought processes that no other dog is able to do. However, I am handicapped in that I am nearly mute. Unfortunately, I do not have the right vocal chords and larynx nor the flexible lips and tongue that go to make up the equipment needed for speech. Everything I want to say, be it calm or full of emotion, comes out:

WOOF!

I heard this gentleman's request for a suitable canine companion and thought, "Here's my chance." I was almost full grown and getting too big for my kennel pen. I was irritated no end by the yappy little Pekinese in the next pen. I was terribly lonesome 'cause it had been a couple of weeks since I last saw my mother and the other puppies in my litter. The food was dull compared to that in my mother's place. So I was itching to make a change. The idea of being a buddy to a little boy sounded so attractive that I put on my act.

"Woof! Woof! Woof!" I said, and I wagged my beautiful collie tail as briskly as I could and smiled my most endearing smile. I even put in a little whine or two, a touch we dogs use to express intense eagerness. I put everything I had into catching the attention of this curious man. The competition to be heard and seen was enormous. Dozens of dogs were barking away, so much so that the keeper had his hands over his ears. But you know what? I got through! There must have been a special tone to my voice, a joyful gesture to my tail, an unusual sweetness to my whine that caught this man's attention.

My keeper and the man with his collar on backward came over to my pen. The keeper explained what my background was, saying, "Here is the absolutely ideal dog to take back to the birthday boy." It was almost as if I had written the script myself! He explained how to feed me and that I had had all my shots against distemper and such. The backward collar man said, "I think this fellow seems to be just what we are looking for" and, reaching into his pocket, he took out a leather leash and collar. The keeper opened my pen and was wise enough to hold me tightly, else I would have leaped upon the gentleman and changed his whole attitude right there. I calmed down enough for my keeper to put the collar on me and attach the leash. He placed the grip in the other man's hand and went over to the desk to get the release papers necessary.

My new master bent over and signed his name with a flourish and then bent over and gave my neck and ears a gentle rub right then and there. He scratched my belly just behind my ribs — my tickle spot! It felt wonderful, as comforting as my mother's tongue. I sensed I was free already and full of expectations that this was going to be the start of a wonderful life.

The keeper and my new master shook hands. I had yet to learn the significance of shaking hands — or rather paws in my case. Then it was:

"Good-bye, Animal Rescue League."

"Thank you, Mr. Keeper."

"Thank you Mr. Collar-on-Backwards" and .... "Hello, Little Boy!"

§§§

WHO AM I?

At this point, I should introduce myself. I'm called Blackface, the name given me by my then five-year-old master. I'm a mutt, not a pure-bred, that sort of dog where the puppies are expected to look exactly like their mother and father. I'm not eligible to be registered with the American Kennel Club. I'll never see "Blackface" on a Certificate of the AKC. Nobody cares who my forebears were, except it's known that I and my litter-mates were the result of a purposeful breeding of a Collie with a Saint Bernard. This breed crossing has been found to produce great child companion dogs, with

4

the intelligence and gentle temperament of my Saint Bernard father and the size and energy of my Collie mother. My coat is like a Collie's and I stand about the same height, but my nose is shorter. I've got the jowls of a St. Bernard, and I'm heavier than a Collie. My ears are like my father's but my bushy tail is like my mother's. My kind really enjoys playing with children 'cause we're sturdy enough to take all the roughhousing that little kids love. And we love the affection that children's' rough-and-tumble represents.

I've heard that people who breed Jack Russell terriers are not interested in registering their dogs with the American Kennel Club because they don't want the breed to be defined by appearance only. Jack Russells are loyal bouncy energy machines that come in both smooth-haired and wiry bodies. Their personality is what distinguishes them. So it is with the Collie-St. Bernard breed I represent. We're bred for our genial tolerant comfortable way we get along with children.

§§§

("As Blackface mentioned before, he sports a remarkable intellect as

*well as the characteristics
expected from his
breeding. That can only
be attributed to a spectacular genetic mutation. I
hope it passes on to many
generations to come!")*

§§§

GOING HOME

Outside the Animal Rescue League was a
brown Studebaker coupe with a rumble seat in
back, a feature that was common on cars built in
the early thirties. When closed, it appeared to be a
car trunk. When opened, it became an unenclosed
forward-facing seat for two, reached by way of foot
pads on the rear fender. It was a breezy place. I
loved sitting there on trips with my master. On this
trip home, however, I was allowed to sit on the
front seat next to the driver and could see the road
up ahead. Oh, joy! Was that ever exciting — my
first trip in a car!

 There were trucks and buses, and milk wag-
ons. There were carts being pulled along by horses.
Big and little automobiles were going in every
direction, with names like Hudson, Willys,

Packard, Nash, DeSoto, and Oldsmobile. It seemed as though every car we passed was an entirely unique vehicle. And there were people in all of them. At the time, I thought it odd that there weren't any dogs doing the driving but I soon realized as I watched my new master manipulate the gear shift lever and pump the several pedals on the floor that we dogs just are not equipped for holding on to the steering wheel or reaching the floor pedals. No hands or ankles.

I only saw one dog the entire trip home and he was nearly falling out the side window of a blue Buick. He was so intent on picking up all the wind-distributed odors and smells that he didn't hear me bark a greeting. I can understand that. When I'm out in a car, I also love to stick my snout out a window to sample all the nice stinky stuff in the air. It's almost impossible to distract me when I'm sniffing with my head out the car window. It's more than just greeting an old friend type of smell. It's like standing on a corner of a busy city street and watching the people go by. There's an endless variety to the parade as it passes, sensed as much through my nostrils as through my eyes — which are half closed anyway as I concentrate on those fascinating nose messages.

We left Brighton and the Animal Rescue League on the west side of Boston. We drove through the streets of Watertown and Waltham onto the roads of Lincoln and Sudbury, eventually leaving behind all but isolated white clapboard farmhouses tucked in amongst the trees. We were way out in the country, enjoying the changing leaves of the maples and the scent of sun-drenched pine. In time, we soon crossed the bridge over the Assabet River into the town of Maynard, our destination.

In those days, Maynard was known world-wide for its large Finnish community and its United Cooperative Society, and its big brick woolen mill. Nowadays, Maynard is a technology town, the former headquarters for Digital, which made-over the old woolen mill buildings for offices and the production of computers. The United Cooperative Society is still in business but nowhere near as important to the town as it used to be. The town fathers had the sense to encourage redevelopment of the down-town shopping area instead of re-zoning the highways for new mega-stores. Downtown Maynard is a busy place, unlike so many towns which have lost their central vitality to the commercial competition set up on cheap land outside town.

But enough of Maynard's appearance. Beyond the Assabet and Main Street, and over the railroad tracks past Nason Street, we turned left around shingled St. George's Episcopal Church onto Florida Road. Finally, we drove into the gravel driveway of a little white Cape Cod cottage and came to a stop. I was frantic to get out and lift my leg before I messed up in the Studebaker and started this whole venture on the wrong foot, the one I would lift to establish my new territory.

My driver, the fellow with his collar on backwards, the Reverend Mr. LaCroix (rhymes with toy), was the minister of that shingled church we just passed. That's why he had his collar on backwards. It seems that that's a mark of an Episcopal minister and also a Catholic priest, although the priest has a narrower piece of collar showing. Mr. LaCroix scurried around to my side of the car just in time to let me out. I leaped out in a rush and sprinkled the mulberry tree next to the driveway long and thoroughly. What relief! My condition was such that it was fortunate I chose a tree. Otherwise, I could have killed a mere bush.

So my life with the LaCroix began.

Boy LaCroix

The white-clapboarded rectory had a screened porch on the driveway side, and two dormer bedrooms over the front. It had a small open entrance porch on the Florida Road side that gave it some sense of formality. Otherwise, it was indistinguishable from hundreds of similar New England dwellings.

The first thing to do, even before entering the house, was to meet my new master, the birthday boy. He had been watching and waiting all morning for his father to return. The minute we pulled into the driveway, he burst forth from the kitchen where his breath had fogged up the window. He didn't see me right away as I was hidden by the Studebaker.

Mr. LaCroix said, "Eldon, I've got a surprise for you. Close your eyes."

Eldon squinted a bit as if his eyes were closed but gave himself away with a loud whoop when he saw me.

"Is he mine, Daddy?"

"You bet. Happy Birthday, fella!" said his father, as Eldon ran to me and threw himself into my furry face.

It was a mutual delight. I slurped my tongue all over his ears and nose and eyes until Eldon couldn't stand it any longer. Fortunately, I was nearly full grown for a dog and he was nice and short for a person, so we could sort of see eye-to-eye.

He'd been given an awful nickname: "Boy." Only his father, when he wanted to get serious, would call him "Eldon." Otherwise, he was always, "Boy." I thought how sad I'd be if my nickname was just "Dog." No distinction at all.

The story goes that when he was born in the rough and crude copper-mining town of Bisbee, Arizona, father LaCroix went up and down the main street at the bottom of the canyon yelling, "It's a boy!" to everyone he saw. "How's the boy?" turned into, "How's Boy?" It stuck. Also, "Eldon" is one of those family names that doesn't make for a good natural nickname like "Bill" or "Tommy" or "Bob."

So "Boy" he became — Boy LaCroix, for the next seven years until Eldon finally rebelled. The worst part was that, as the names rhymed, everybody thought it was cute. Boy just hated being thought of as cute. I could feel his fists clench tight whenever someone said, "Oh! This is Boy. Boy LaCroix. How cute!"

§§§

("Eldon speaking. I'm writing all this down as it is told to me. Obviously, Blackface — furry paws and all — is unable to write. Do you remember that time I tried to get you to write

11

*your name? It looked
like a dozen caterpillars
dipped in ink had a party
on the paper! You were
absolutely right, Black-
face! It used to make me
cringe to be called "Boy"
all the time. I envied my
school chums with
traditional nicknames.
The older I got, the more
the name "Boy" irritated
me.")*

§§§

House Rules

Inasmuch as the nickname stuck, that's
what I'll call you in this story: Boy. That's the name
I knew you by most of my life. You had brown
hair on your head like mine and big brown eyes
like mine and we liked each other immediately. I
slobbered all over your face every time we greeted
each other — you tasted nice and salty. Your
mother didn't seem to like dog kisses, though. She
washed your face right away when she saw me
slobbering on her child.

I quickly found out that big people didn't appreciate it at all when I got up on my hind legs to greet them face to face. This business of putting my paws on their chest became the ultimate "no-no." Seems as though the problem was not that I stood tall but that my dirty feet got on their clean clothes. Mr. LaCroix found that by crossing his arms low in front, he would effectively block my upward surge. I eventually got the message when my muzzle began to hurt from the repeated self-inflicted battering. With you and your friends, we were on the same level to start with.

As you know, dogs don't need shoes. We have spongy pads on our paws for a wearing surface, and the tops are all covered with fur for insulation. Unfortunately, we do pick up mud and stuff that sticks to the fur on our paws. Mrs. LaCroix especially would check my feet before she would let me in the house. She got tired of swabbing the kitchen floor every time I came in from the muddy yard. She bought one of those diagonal stick gates for the dining room doorway so the carpets beyond would stay free of muddy paw prints.

Another thing that I had to adjust to was the way people ate. Instead of a sturdy bowl on the floor so you could get your nose down close to the food, taste and smell being so connected. You people put food on flat plates on a high table. Then you sit on chairs and use metal sticks to pick up the food and carry it to your mouths. That seems like a lot of unnecessary trouble, just to eat food. Think of all the joy of smell you miss that way!

I have to admit here and now that I envy you people with your flexible fingers and opposable thumb. You can grab, you can scoop, and you can point. I can't do any of those things. But what I envy the most is this: you can scratch your own rump!

If you have ever watched a dog closely as he tries to ease an itch or bite a flea, you know the strange contortions we have to perform to reach much of our bodies. Our leg sockets permit forward and back movement but we can't move them sideways. You have full movement of both arms and legs. You can make angels in the snow, stand spread-eagled, and can swing your arms around to touch all but the very top center of your back. There's one advantage I have that you can't match though — not that you would ever find it useful. I can bite my belly.

The table the LaCroix ate from was just a bit too high for me to peer over, so I never could see what exactly it was they ate. I would get the scraps from the table later in my bowl, but by then the initial pungency had pretty much evaporated and the texture changed. It was forbidden to feed me from the table.

Late and cold or not, I appreciated those table scraps. They added surprise and variety to my diet. I was generally fed out in the back pantry, where I also had a big water bowl, and where I bedded down for the night when I wasn't in Boy's room. It was the place where I had to go when there were other people in the house who didn't like dogs or were allergic to dog hair. I've found that there are very few people who really do not like us dogs. There are, however, many people who are afraid of dogs and I can sense that fear. When I do, it's best I just make myself scarce and head back to the pantry.

§§§

("You really had a time of it, didn't you, getting used to playing by the rules that people set up for dogs. I never thought of it like that. I always thought that dogs just did dog things. It never crossed my mind that dogs had to learn a new set of "behavior rules." Kennel rules were easier!")

§§§

15

We got along very well, the LaCroix family and I. Well, occasionally I would get in trouble, like the first time I did some digging in the sweet soft dirt in Mrs. LaCroix's flower bed. The ground felt good, and the freshly-turned dirt and flowers smelled heavenly. But Mrs. LaCroix got very angry at me for getting in there and digging a resting spot. She shooed me off with a rolled-up newspaper. I slunk away to the creek to lie with my head between my paws and wonder what I'd done wrong. I think it was my digging in that particular spot 'cause I could dig in the field after mice and moles and nobody objected. I also found out the hard way that peeing on bushes around the house was not appreciated. Trees are all right, and fire plugs and sign posts and telephone poles, but not azaleas.

The worst thing I did that first year with the LaCroix was an accident, and I wasn't really responsible for it, though I felt awful afterward. Mr. LaCroix or someone had stored a big cast-iron radiator in the back pantry, and one day, Boy and I were roughhousing out there and I brushed up against this loose cast-iron monster and knocked it over on Boy's ankle. It pinned him there and he started to cry and call for his mother — loud and with anxiety in the tone. She quickly came and moved that heavy radiator off Boy's ankle. She lifted Boy up and hurried off to the Studebaker to take Boy to the hospital emergency room.

Boy's ankle was broken. His leg was put in a hard white sleeve and he hobbled about for weeks on crutches. He couldn't run at all. However, I could help him get around. He would lean on me and with my four good legs and his one, and we could move about pretty well. We might have bumped into the furniture some, but we didn't break anything that my tail wouldn't have hit anyway. I had a hard time in the beginning learning when and where it was safe to express my feelings with a vigorous tail-wag.

Another problem I had was the difference between the kind of smells I liked and those Mrs. LaCroix thought were nice. Now, there's nothing more delightful to us dogs than rolling around in something rotten like old manure. Maybe you know how neat an old manure pile smells, one that's been sitting long enough for the bacteria to have broken down all the ammonia and raw organisms? Well, Mrs. LaCroix thought that smell was awful. You would have thought I had smallpox the way she treated me after I rolled around in one of those neat stinkpiles, or over a good old dead fish. Slam went the door. "Shoo!" went the voice. I knew I'd done wrong again but I wasn't sure what rule I had violated. Repetition of the stink and banishment routine was the only way I could

17

know. Often, Boy would be instructed to hose me off. I had to be really careful what I rolled on in order to avoid being shut out of doors and away from the family.

§§§

("That broken ankle was a real bother. I think the crutches hurt my arm sockets more than the ankle hurt. Having you around to lean on instead of using the crutches was great. Thanks! And when you got banished, it was just as hard on me. You were my closest friend.")

§§§

GREEN DOOR

It wasn't just me that got into mischief, believe me. I think the worst was Boy's doing, but it happened before I ever joined the family. It was such a wild tale I must have heard the LaCroix tell it on Boy a dozen times. Seems that the doors to the church's parish hall were getting a new coat of green paint one summer. At noon, the painters went home for lunch and left their paint cans and brushes behind. Boy was playing in the sandbox, watching the painters, and when they left, he decided he too was going to paint the doors. So he picked up a brush in his little four-year-old hands and began swishing away with this green oil paint. Some spattered on his clothes. He took them off. More spattered on his skin. He thought that was sort of neat so he shifted his attention from the door to his own body and painted himself all green.

The workers at the woolen mill came by on their way back from lunch and were having an hilarious time watching this little naked tyke paint himself green. Mrs. LaCroix heard this strange laughter and came out just as Boy was finishing the job. Can you imagine how she felt?

I'm told it took quarts of turpentine and hours to clean Boy up, and some very sheepish painters got a super tongue-lashing for being so careless with their paint. I'm glad I wasn't around then or I, too, would have been painted green.

You have heard of hot-dogs, yellow-dog Democrats, and red-dog line play, but "green-dog" has yet to enter the language.

§§§

("You weren't there or sure as rain, I'd have painted you green too. That wasn't the only mischief I got into. My first spanking came when I took my great grand-father's cane outdoors and lost the engraved gold head. It was a unique cane that had 'j-e-f-f-e-r-s-o-n d-a-v-i-s' carved on each smooth oval where a twig had been cut from the stalk that formed the cane. Now, that I remember all too well!")

§§§

Ice Boxes

Technology has really changed since I was a young pup. You wouldn't believe the difference between life for you now and life for me in 1930. For instance, when someone forgot to refill my water bowl, I could always get a nice cool drink from the drip pan under the ice box. You see, refrigerators were just beginning to become ordinary household appliances. Most people had big wooden insulated cabinets — ours was in the back pantry where I slept — where each week, a man would come in to the house with a big black rubber sheet over his shoulder. He would be carrying a huge block of ice with metal tongs and place it in the ice box so food could be stored there without going bad. When you wanted some ice for a cool summer drink, you would use an ice pick to chip off a piece of the big block to fit into your glass.

Everyone had a square cardboard sign that had "5," "10," "20," and "30" printed on its four edges. You put it in your front window the day the iceman was due to come by, with the number of pounds you wanted facing up. He could read your order from the street and cut up the right size chunk in his wagon. He had to brush sawdust off the surface that came from the icehouse insulation before he delivered the ice. I loved to greet the iceman if I could, 'cause he often left lots of sweet cool chips in the gutter for me to lick.

§§§

("You know, it is really remarkable how the usual pace of life has changed with the advances in technology. Even for a dog, the changes are spectacular. For instance, there's now a way to prevent rabies or distemper. There are medicines that get rid of intestinal worms that used to plague all you dogs. Even the fight against fleas has been won!")

§§§

The LaCroix family had a radio in those days. Television hadn't been invented yet. You had to use your imagination to picture what was going on while the sounds were coming in over the airwaves. This particular ancient radio was run on DC current. Instead of being plugged into the house electric sockets, it had a big wet storage battery in a cabinet under it. I didn't much like the smell of the radio battery acid, but I liked listening to the radio sounds, such as the Lone Ranger's horse whinnying, or a wolf howling in the background. It made me want to howl back. I'd cock my head to one side, much like the spotted terrier that RCA used as their symbol.

That RCA dog had ears that stand up and look alert, but mine always droop no matter how hard I try to lift them. It makes me look sort of slow-witted, but there's nothing I can do about it. Some kids can wiggle their ears and some can't. Some of us dogs just have permanent earmuffs.

What I howled at the most was the Victrola. It was an early version of a record player that didn't work on electricity. You had to wind it up for the record disc to revolve. These were big thick platters of black brittle stuff and the sound they produced was terribly tinny by today's standards. That was the state of the art in 1930. When

Mrs. LaCroix would put on a record of people singing what she called "opera," I was always banished to the back pantry, 'cause I would start howling every time Caruso sang. Boy thought it was because I wanted to join in the singing too, but it was really because the sound from the Victrola bothered my sensitive ears.

§§§

("Blackface, you're lucky. When I was at boarding school and living away from you, I came to love Big Band music played very loud with lots of trumpet and piercing clarinet. You would have been frantic if I had played Benny Goodman's **'Sing, Sing, Sing'** *around you.")*

§§§

HEALTH FADS

People had fads and beliefs in 1930 that might seem both odd and familiar today. For instance, Mrs. LaCroix had Boy sleep out in the open in winter, on the screened porch. It was supposed to be good for you, breathing fresh air at night. So Mrs. LaCroix would have Boy all bundled up under blankets and comforters so just his little nose poked out. I was allowed to sleep out there with him, but I had to lie on the cold floor and would much rather stay in the back pantry. After all, Saint Bernards aren't left outdoors in the snow all the time. We appreciate the warmth of an open fire just as much as people do, after an afternoon of romping in the snow with Boy and his friends.

At the breakfast table, there was granulated honey in a big tin instead of sugar, and there was hot oatmeal over which the LaCroix family sprinkled a health food called silloway seed. It was supposed to keep you "regular" — made sure you pooped.

Brown eggs were thought to be better than white ones, and the bread was all made at home rather than being bought. Mr. LaCroix had the job of getting my food ready, and he was pretty good about making table scraps into a tasty stew. He was a lot more reliable than Boy would have been, so I had no complaints on that account. Canned dog food hadn't become commonplace, so Mr. LaCroix would often pick up a big ham bone from the butcher for me to chew on.

That's a treat that dogs these day seldom enjoy. People are now afraid that the bits of sharp bone we produce while gnawing on a bone will puncture our intestines. They may be right, but dogs have been gnawing on bones long before they became man's hunting companions. A bone to me is like a banana split to you.

§§§

("I have to say you were either lucky or have a very tough gut. I've seen a good canine friend die from eating chicken bones thrown away on a construction site. Guthrie — a companion to all my children later on — died in extreme pain from a punctured intestine. Brittle bones are very bad news for dogs.")

§§§

It might be hard for you to realize it but people went to the market nearly every day to buy food. There weren't any supermarkets in 1930. As I mentioned before, there were very few refrigerators, and they couldn't hold very much. So off to the stores people would go everyday to buy food. There wasn't any frozen food. There weren't any special chemicals added to the food to keep it from spoiling fast. The only ways one could preserve food was to can it, pickle it, salt it, or put it up as preserves in glass jars. Packaging of anything other than dry food like cereal was nearly non-existent. And, most likely, you walked to and from the stores with your purchases. That limited what you could buy on one trip to what you could carry.

There were many small shops instead of one big food store. The butcher sold meat. The fish-monger sold fresh fish. The green-grocer sold fruits and vegetables. In winter time, he was hard put to keep his store stocked and sold dried fruit and root vegetables that would keep: potatoes, beets, parsnips, and carrots. Other vegetables that wouldn't spoil such as hard squash, cabbage, and cauliflower could also be found. Special green-house-grown produce he might have now and then for very high prices. And a shipment of oranges from Florida was a rare and expensive item.

There was a dairy store that sold milk, butter, cheese, eggs, and peanut butter. Peanut butter and butter were kept in big tubs. You scooped out what you wanted into the same sort of waxed cardboard box that you get Chinese carry-outs in today. The grocery store sold staples such as flour and sugar, as well as boxed and canned products. Dry foods like flour, beans, rice, and sugar were sold by weight. A clerk would scoop out of a barrel what you wanted, dump it into a paper sack, and weigh it on a hanging scale. He would get each purchase for you. There was no self-service, no metal carts to push around. It was not at all unusual for known customers to put purchases "on the tab" and have them delivered by a young man on a bicycle.

The hardware store sold, in addition to tools and nails, cleaning equipment and soaps. Downtown was full of little specialty food shops. I wasn't allowed to go inside any of the food shops. I liked to sit outside the butcher shop and look hungry. Often, one of the butchers would throw me a scrap or two. And I liked to go into the hardware store to sniff around. As you know, we dogs are very sensitive to smell. You people may learn a lot through your eyes, but we dogs are great at using our noses. I could tell what season it was without looking. All I had to do was stick my nose into the hardware store. Spring smelled of grass seed. Summer smelled of bone meal. Fall smelled

of gunpowder, and winter smelled of oiled leather
and kerosene.

§§§

> (*"You know, Blackface, I
> do believe you lived at a
> great time for dogs. The
> manufactured dog food
> now available in stores
> is just plain awful. My
> father probably prepared
> the best tasting most
> healthful food you could
> have, anywhere and at
> anytime. [Except for those
> ham bones!]"*)

§§§

Of course, we also have far better hearing than people do. Did you know that we dogs can hear sound vibrations pitched much higher than even a treble choirboy can produce or even hear? There are special whistles made that make sound over 20,000 hertz that only dogs can hear. Pealing church bells can produce overtones that are painful to dogs and to our sensitive ears. You people might think some sounds are just beautiful, but those same sounds drive us dogs to distraction.

I've mentioned how Mrs. LaCroix and I differ on what smells good and what stinks. The same goes for taste. I love to gnaw on a bone, even an old bone. I can eat and digest old rotten food you would gag at. I like that hard commercial dogfood you call kibble, and I also like horsemeat and whatever else they throw into canned dogfood — stuff I know people turn up their noses at. I stick my nose in just about everything that's put in my food bowl and wolf it down with gusto!

Except — some things you people eat with pleasure, I would push aside, even if you put it into my bowl. Such things as fresh tomatoes, apples, squash, pumpkin, broccoli, and other similar vegetation I avoid. You might have noticed what the dogs in your neighborhood do when they feel sick. They go and eat grass. We dogs think of vegetation as medicine. However, you, dear reader,

are not a dog. You should eat your broccoli and
Brussel sprouts, your kale and collard greens, your
parsnips, eggplant, and onions and spinach. Those
vegetables are good for you, but they are not for me!

§§§

*("You forgot turnips! As
for your wonderful hear-
ing ability, I can remember
times in Maynard when my
mother would go outside in
winter to call us in for
supper. I couldn't hear a
thing. She was out of earshot for me. You, however,
would stop, your head
would turn just a bit, your
floppy ears would flare out,
and you would come over
and tug at my sleeve. That
was a clear sign I should
stop sledding and look.
There would be my mother
over across Florida Road,
waving her arms off in the
distance. You had uncanny
hearing ability.")*

§§§

Getting back to smells, let me give you a good example. There was the time Boy came home from school one afternoon when he was in the first grade. I was good at sensing time, even without a wrist watch on my leg. I had gotten into the habit of trotting east about two in the afternoon and greeting Boy a couple of blocks from home. I would walk back with him, checking out the neighborhood cats and squirrels as we went. One afternoon, I sensed something was wrong. Boy was sort of sidling along the sidewalk with his legs held very close together. When we were ten dog-lengths apart, I knew what was the matter. My nose told me! He had not been able to hold back and had pooped in his shorts on the way home. Obviously, he was uncomfortable, and I sensed he was ashamed (We dogs can sense feelings pretty well too). Fortunately, no other children were along that day so we were able to get home and to the care and assistance of Mrs. LaCroix without further embarrassment. She was most gentle and sympathetic. Another mother with less patience might have gotten mad and punished the boy. But Mrs. LaCroix took it in stride and that made me feel good, too.

Poor Boy's predicament reminded me of the misery and trouble I went through myself, getting housebroken. That was a terribly hard lesson for me to learn — that dogs were not supposed to lift their leg on the dining room table or leave a nice neat dry pile of lumps on the living room rug. As I saw it, the table leg was the next best thing to a tree I could find inside the house, and the rug was the closest thing indoors to a stretch of grass. Neither impression was right by people standards. It took a lot of painful learning for me to know that the only place I could relieve myself was outdoors, even in the coldest winter.

There's a phrase I've heard, "I wouldn't do it to a dog." It's always in reference to something miserable. Well, I perfectly well understand.

§§§

("I understand as well. Most of the time, I got the dickens for being there and not stopping you when you did something gross. But thank you now for your sympathy when I pooped in my shorts. I was deathly afraid I'd meet somebody on the street who knew me. What an embarrassment that would have been.")

§§§

As I mentioned in the beginning, I'm half Saint Bernard. Those early Saint Bernards got their name from the monastery where they were first bred. These were big dogs, with extra thick coats, very little exposed nose, good hearing and sense of smell. They were very strong, reliable, and gentle. The monks would tie a little keg around the dog's neck filled with liquid nourishment and send the dogs out in snowstorms to find lost travelers. They were also good at finding and digging out people who had become buried by avalanches. If a dog found some person in trouble, he would cuddle up, offer the keg, and howl to bring help. It is a great legacy I try to maintain.

The other half of me stems from the sheep-herding dogs of Scotland. Collies are sharp-nosed and lean, though they look heavier because they have a fur coat that fluffs out and doesn't hug the body. Their long full tails look like hearth brooms, and their ears are cocked high on their heads. A good sheep dog has to be lean with lots of stamina to handle all the running around it takes to herd sheep. They herd animals by instinct. This ability to control and manage a herd of sheep is very valuable.

A good sheep dog allows a shepherd to cover miles of ground and hundreds of animals he could never manage alone. It takes a very smart dog to read and understand the shepherd's gestures — or whistles — at a distance and anticipate the next move of the sheep and head them off.

I claim my father's physical attributes of temperament and size, my mother's brains and stamina. There must be a modicum of herding instinct in me also. I love to chase flocks of pigeons in the park. As for my remarkable level of intelligence, I think it has to have been a mutation of the collie sheep dog smart gene. There was something there to start with.

§§§

("Your reference to instinct is something that interests me greatly. How does It work? Do you have some sort of weird computer software in your DNA that directs it to react in a specific way when confronted with a herd of sheep? I can see genes passing on physical

35

characteristics like noses and hair color. It's magic when bits of DNA can determine the shape of an Oriole's pendant nest.")

§§§

CHAPTER TWO: MAYNARD

IN WHICH I LEARN
ABOUT DEATH AND LIFE

SNOW AND MAPLE LEAVES

Collie and Saint Bernard: those are very demanding family traditions I was expected to live up to. Although I seldom had a chance to rescue anybody, when the opportunity arose I was up to it.

I loved to play in the snow with Boy and his friends. The cold didn't bother me at all, and I could chase after the kids when they went sledding on the hill across Florida Road. They would often go down the hill in a cardboard box, winter on snow and summer on grass — the box made a great toboggan. And I would jump in on top of everybody when they got to the bottom. I didn't enjoy actually riding downhill. It frightened me not to be in control. But the fun of rough-housing in the snow at the bottom was what I enjoyed the most.

As far as exhibiting my Collie heritage, I can say that when the opportunity came to herd sheep, I was up to that too — except it was not appreciated and I got in trouble doing it.

I liked to roughhouse in the maple leaves in the fall. Boy and I would go for a long walk up to Libby's house. She was a few years older than Boy but they liked to play together and their parents saw a lot of each other as well. Libby lived on a street lined with large sugar maples and in October, you couldn't see the ground for the leaves. We wouldn't walk where we thought the sidewalk was. It was more fun to shuffle through the gutter, where the dry leaves were often piled to twice my shoulder height. Boy would leap into the biggest piles and sink out of sight. With my Saint Bernard nose, I could always find him, even when nobody else could.

§§§

"My
coat's
a lot
warmer
than
Boy's."

Libby's street full of leaves triggers another memory. It was standard practice in the Thirties for people to rake their leaves into piles, and then set fire to them. Fall in Maynard smelled of burning leaves for a month. A gray layer of leaf smoke hung over the town on windless days. The smoke was fragrant, but it was really bad for people with allergies and lung problems, and for air quality in general. People didn't know anything about the hazards of pollution in the Thirties. Tobacco smoke was so thick in some indoor spaces you would choke trying to breathe. Nobody gave it a thought. The health hazards of cigarette smoking were unknown.

About 1980, the practice of burning leaves was stopped by law in most towns and now all those leaves get picked up and carried away. In well-run towns, they are recycled and transformed into useful mulch and plant food. In other places, leaves are a waste product clogging up the landfills. There aren't any more head-high piles of maple leaves for children and dogs to play in but the air is much cleaner in the fall, even with the increased production of carbon monoxide, nitrous oxide, and sulphur dioxide that pour out of the exhausts of cars. Those are some smells I am ready do without!

§§§

*("Well Blackface, you
certainly have learned a
lot about ecology and air
pollution. I'm impressed.
Not only does car exhaust
smell bad, it causes many
people to have asthma
attacks, and the stuff
floats upwards and
combines with other nasty
gasses. That chemical
reaction produces what
is called by scientists the
'greenhouse effect.' Solar
radiation reflected off the
ground is in turn reflected
back to Earth from this
layer of gases, heating our
globe. Bad news for furry
critters like you. But you
knew all that.")*

§§§

THE CHOW

The first time I went with Boy over to Libby's, we went the shortest way, and coming back, we were challenged by a big fuzzy red dog with a black mouth and a tail that curled up over his back like a doughnut. I found out later that he was a Chow, of Chinese ancestry. Anyway, this Chow growled some nasty things to me, something about the sidewalk right here was his and I couldn't get by and my mother was a pig. A pig! He knew perfectly well my mother was no pig! He insulted my mother and I felt I had to respond for honor's sake. Besides, he was about my size so I figured he couldn't hurt me. I was wrong, very very wrong!

This Chow was a professional fighter and he went for my legs before I knew what was happening. His fur was so dense I couldn't get a purchase on his neck, and his teeth were really digging into my leg, as if he was trying to break the bone inside. Panic struck. Boy was yanking on my tail, trying to pull us apart. With one last furious growl, I manage to twist away and bolt for home. I learned then that I wasn't the fighter I thought I was. Each and every time afterwards when we went to Libby's, we took the long way round. I didn't live to the ripe old age of sixteen without knowing when to fight and when to duck out.

§§§

*("The idea that avoiding
a fight is something only
for sissies is so stupid!
You were right. The smart
thing is always to use
one's reasoning ability
to solve differences of
opinion. Of course, some
folk don't have any
reasoning ability. In that
case, ducking out is the
intelligent way to go.")*

§§§

Summer Hill

Not all the dogs I ran into were as mean
as that Chow. Gordon was Boy's best friend in
Maynard, and Gordon's little dog Giant and I got
along very well, even though he was a third my
size. We would tag along when our masters would
go exploring on Summer Hill, up behind Gordon's

house. There was a big boulder there that the boys said was made of fool's gold. It had shiny flakes on it that you could break off and pretend were real pirate gold.

We would play tag in the overgrown meadow on the hill, which was often a problem for me later. I would pick up huge clots of burrs from the weeds that grew in the field. These burrs were round fuzzy balls with tiny hooks on them, just like those on Velcro. Boy would take hours when we got home, picking those burrs off me before Mrs. LaCroix would let me in the house again. Those burrs would also stick to Boy's corduroy knickers and wool stockings and even his shoe-laces.

Young boys didn't wear long pants in the Thirties. They wore knickers, pants that just went down just over the knee and closed tightly over long stockings that came up to the knee. Golfers used to wear similar pants called "plus-fours" — and I haven't the least clue as to why they were called that.

Back to burrs. Burrs were a lot easier to pick off cloth than out of my heavy fur. After Boy got all the burrs out, he would take a metal comb and pull it through my fur and scrape across my skin below, clearing every tangle and satisfying every itch. Then he would give my coat a nice brushing, which brought out the luster. It was worth putting up with the burrs to get such wonderful treatment.

44

§§§

("If I remember correctly,
you got your tickle spot
rubbed a lot during the
de-burring process, too.
Burrs got into my hair as
well as yours, you know.
That was the worst part
for me, having my mother
pull out hair along with
the burrs.")

§§§

ASSABET RIVER

Some dogs like water and some don't. My
attitude toward water is that it's something nice
to lap up and maybe to wade in, but you would
seldom get me leaping into a lake for the joy of it.
That may be all right for hunting dogs like
Chesapeake Bay Retrievers and Newfoundlands,

and for some smaller fellows like Corgis and
Springer Spaniels, but, as I say, water is to drink.
And to play in only when it's in the form of snow.

Boy, Gordon, Giant and I would often go up
the Summer Hill dirt road and on to the Assabet
River before it flowed through the town. The river
picked up a foul discharge from the woolen mill
further on downstream. But on the west edge of
town, the river ran in a wide rock-strewn series of
shallow pools and riffles. There were occasional
tires and cans and stuff that thoughtless people
had thrown into the water, but the water itself
was clear and sweet. In the pools, there were fish I
would pounce on but never could catch, and there
were crawfish the boys would uncover by turning
over rocks in the river bed.

Upstream from the place we always went
was a steel truss bridge that took Summer Hill
Road over the river. It marked the limit past which
neither Boy nor Gordon were permitted to go. But
that was fine because another Gordon — we called
him Gordo — lived in a house that backed up to
the part of the river we always played in. He and
his dog Dolo would often come join us, and it got
pretty merry when all six of us got to splashing
each other. Of course, that sort of thing didn't sit
very well with Mrs. LaCroix or Gordon's mother
when we all got home. Boy might get a scolding
and have to put on dry clothes. I would get
banished to the yard to dry off. It seems that

my fur starts to smell bad to certain people when
it gets wet. Funny, but I think it's a great smell
— like the odor given off by a wet wool sweater.

§§§

("Do I like the smell of
wet wool? Frankly, No.
And I didn't enjoy walking
home all wet in the fall
when the wind would cut
through my wet clothes
and start me to shivering.
It never seemed to bother
you, though. That's
because you have a forest
of dense short hairs next
to your skin that keeps
you dry and warm.")

§§§

Ordinarily, Boy was restricted to a rather small area of Maynard, but there were three places I haven't mentioned yet that he and I were allowed to go. One was to Dickie's house, another was to Annabelle's house, and the last was to Frankie's place. These kids were all classmates of Boy's at the Roosevelt Grammar School on Nason Street.

Dickie's father was a doctor and had his office on the ground floor of their house downtown. There wasn't much yard to play in and so most activity went on inside. I got to see Dickie's playroom in the attic the first time I went there — before his mother told Dickie I had to stay outside — and I can see why. That playroom was huge and filled with big toys.

There was something called an Irish Mail up there, a cart you could ride on and move by pulling a handle back and forth. Only Dickie had any mastery of this contraption because it was hard to pump and steer at the same time. I was run into several times because I could never tell which way it might lurch next. Imagine riding one of those contraptions inside the house. Gives you an idea how much space there was in Dickie's attic playroom.

I remember getting to eat the left-over Spaghetti-Os when Dickie's mother fed all the kids lunch one day. I liked Dickie's mother a lot, even if

I had to stay outside. I confess to being something of a glutton, and anyone that feeds me has won my undying loyalty and affection. Do you share my enthusiasm for Spaghetti-Os, or is it just me?

Annabelle was a girl. She wore dresses. She didn't like dogs, and she was no fun to play with. However, she lived near Boy's friend Earl and was part of a group of kids that came home from school together. She also took piano lessons from the same teacher as Boy, so he would go over to Annabelle's house to practice duets and I would follow along. Duets are musical pieces played by two people at the same time on one piano — one plays the treble notes, the other plays the bass. With four hands times five fingers, it can produce an awful lot of notes and noise.

At first, I could go in on the porch where the piano was. But after the time I joined in and howled when they banged the keys and played too loud — it hurt my ears — I had to stay outside at Annabelle's as well as at Dickies.

Annabelle wasn't Boy's favorite girl. There were two others he liked better: Marian, who he thought was the prettiest girl in his class at school and left him tongue-tied when she came around, and Natalie, who lived up near Gordon. Natalie was one of the gang, a regular tomboy. Natalie liked to hug and pet me too, so I grew particularly fond of her.

I wondered for a while why Natalie wasn't coming by the house to walk to school with Boy. I learned she died of leukemia. It made me very sad that summer of 1932. It just didn't seem fair for a neat person like Natalie to have had such a short life. It took me a long time to accept the fact that good people can die young and through no fault of their own. If someone runs out in the street without looking and gets hit by a car and gets killed, that's one thing. Natalie's death didn't make any sense.

In contrast, life blossomed and billowed at Frankie's. His father was a shoemaker and didn't make a lot of money. Their house was small and unpainted, and there were lots of kids in the family. It was always a joyful time when I went to Frankie's with Boy. Someone was always ready to pet me 'cause they didn't have a dog in the family. Everyone wanted to feed me something, and I went for the little sausage bits especially. It seems that there was something always simmering on the stove, throwing off exquisite odors.

If it wasn't for my being pals with Boy, I think I would have preferred to live at Frankie's. You may be too young to know how smells can conjure up vivid memories of places and times, but the smell of Italian cooking brings back those trips to Frankie's and makes me drool.

§§§

("Natalie's death hung in my mind for a long time. I didn't witness her dying. There wasn't any vivid memory there to keep recurring. It was just so — puzzling. More moving to me was seeing Libby's older brother just before he died. I went with my father when he went visiting, and I can still see Jimmie's face in my mind's eye. It was strangely and reassuringly calm. He knew he was dying and had accepted the fact.")

§§§

One of my favorite things to do was to be taken on an excursion to Sudbury to visit the Wayside Inn. I would get to ride in the rumble seat with Boy while Mr. and Mrs. LaCroix rode inside. I could sniff all those tantalizing odors that float across the countryside and guess what they might mean. Boy would keep a tight hold on me the whole trip, I guess to make sure I didn't fall out in my eagerness to smell each and every odor riding on the wind.

The Wayside Inn is more than just an old carriage stop on the Boston to New York Post Road. It was a place where travelers in Colonial times could have a meal and stay the night. In those days, Sudbury was a full day's ride from Boston for the stage coach. It's become an historical park, put together by Henry Ford.

There was the Inn, where I was never allowed inside. Then across the road was the carriage house. This place held several Colonial carriages and smelled of leather and horse manure, a beautiful treat for a sensitive nose like mine. These carriages had leather straps for springs, big wooden-spoked wheels taller than Boy, with narrow iron tires, and a bench sticking out from the front of the roof for the driver. In front of each carriage was a wooden pole to which four horses would be tethered, two on each side.

The carriages themselves didn't take up much space, but the wooden shafts made it necessary to build a much longer carriage house than you might expect, a lot deeper than the building one needs to house a car. When I was there, they uncoupled the shafts to house two carriages in one long stall. There were other buildings in the Wayside Inn complex, some there originally, some moved there from other places. In between, the area was kept as an open park with a rural feel. Instead of motor-driven lawnmowers, they relied on sheep to keep the grass cropped.

§§§

("Inside the Wayside
Inn where you weren't
allowed, the ghost of
Longfellow wandered.
He had written a book
about it. There were
18th Century initials
scratched on an old
windowpane and all the
old floorboards creaked.
The food served in the

dining room was l8th
Century fare, and the staff
went around in costume. If
mutton was on the menu,
it was probably one of
those sheep you chased.")

§§§

SHEEP

Remember my mentioning that my Collie background got me in trouble? Beyond the carriage house was the sheepcote, a low shed in a field that gave the flock some protection in bad weather. The Ford people kept this flock of sheep, not only to give keep the grass clipped, but also to add historical authenticity to the place and be part of a domestic zoo. Most of the times we went to the Wayside Inn I was on a leash, because of what happened the first time I went there.

I'm embarrassed to say so, but I went joyfully wild at the sight of all these shaggy animals about my size and went charging off toward the herd, barking "Hello" as best I could.

This had to have been my Collie heritage coming to the fore, wouldn't you say? Anyway, my action frightened the sheep something awful and they began running in all directions away from me. I thought they would be happy to meet and play with me but I was very much mistaken! I guess those sheep must have already been chased by other dogs who weren't as polite as I am. I started to circle them and head them back to the sheepcote instinctively, barking commands as I went.

The shepherd heard the commotion and came running. He chewed out Mr. LaCroix pretty harshly for letting me run loose and nearly "killing" his precious sheep. Of course I had no intention at all of hurting those stupid sheep. But I have to admit, it was fun to see them run. Now I have to be content just to look at them from the safety of my leash.

Beyond the sheepcote was the Old Stone Mill, a working mill with millpond, raceway, and water wheel, set out in the middle of a grassy valley. It had its own great smell, a mix of lubricating oil, wheat flour, and ground corn. You could hear the dull rumble of the granite grindstones inside as they turned on each other to transform hard corn nibblets into cornmeal. If you like cornbread — and I certainly do when its in my leftover stew — then this is the sort of place that makes it. I like any place that produces good things to eat.

§§§

*("That Wayside Inn mill
was one of the few left
that work. Once, the
mill in America was the
center of industry in an
agricultural society. They
were all water-powered,
with a great big wheel on
the outside turned by the
flow of a running stream.
There was usually a man-
made dam to control the
flow. The water-wheel
revolved, and by a set of
gears that transferred the
motion, the grindstone
turned slowly. Eventually,
water power gave way to
coal-fired steam and then
to electricity.")*

§§§

Mary's Little Lamb

You surely have heard that poem about a girl named Mary who had a pet lamb, the one that followed her to school one day. Well, that poem was based on reality and the reality is on the Wayside Inn grounds: the very one-room red schoolhouse where "it made the children laugh and play to see the lamb at school." I wonder if it was against the rules to take a dog to school in those days. I know I was welcome at the schools Boy went to only under very limited circumstances.

§§§

("Every time I let you inside my school, it was a mob scene. Everyone wanted to pet you, remember? That's why schools don't encourage dogs, except for seeing-eye dogs. They're trained to lie quietly beside their masters. Now, that's something you do

automatically, eh?
[Only when you are so
tired it's not worth your
while to show your usual
independence].")

§§§

GENERAL STORE

Another place I especially liked was the
general store. They would let me inside this place,
where the odors made for exquisite sniffing. There
would be hams hanging from the rafters, barrels
of feed grains, dried fish, crackers, pickles, and
apples. There was a case full of old-fashioned
candy. Boy would stand in front of it for minutes
at a time, trying to make up his mind about which
goodies to choose with his five pennies. In those
days, a nickel could get you enough candy to make
you sick. Boy liked best the little wax figures with
sweet liquid inside. He could chew the wax long
after the nectar went. There were long strips of
paper with little dots of candy stuck on like polka-
dots, rubbery sticks of licorice, sticky gum drops,

and clumps of rock candy that had crystallized on a string. Today, all the store candy is wrapped and labeled, and a penny might get you a single jelly bean. At the Wayside Inn general store, though, five cents could produce a big smile on Boy, and a stomach-ache as well.

§§§

("I never liked the licorice. There were also red cherries inside a liquid-filled chocolate shell but they cost too much. You were right. It was awfully hard to decide as I fingered the few pennies in my pocket.")

§§§

REV. LaCROIX

Often Boy's father would ask me, "Do you want to go visiting?" Of course! This was his invitation to accompany him on rounds to visit shut-in and sick parishioners. I enjoyed these visits, not only for the ride but because everyone doted on me and usually had some snack ready. These trips were usually in broad daylight.

Regularly, I would be asked after dark if I wanted to go for a ride. It was an invitation to provide company for Boy's father when he drove over to Concord. There he would meet with another minister who had collected food and clothing for us to bring back to Maynard. Concord was better situated to weather the Great Depression than Maynard. On many an occasion, the Russian Orthodox priest would accompany us. He was one of Rev. LaCroix's close friends and had the same needs for his parishioners as did the Rector of St. George's. The woolen mill was the main employer in Maynard and many workers were either immigrants from Midland England or the Russian Ukraine.

I would do night rides with these two "men-of-the-cloth" as they distributed under cover of darkness much needed food and clothing to families of men who would have but a half-day shift per week at the mill. It would have been embarrassing to have one's neighbors know that such assistance was necessary. But everyone we visited had a kind word and a pat on the head for me, a sort of dignified indirect thank-you for Mr. LaCroix and the Russian priest.

§§§

*("It seems strange
hearing about these trips
from you. I never was
asked to go on these trips
of mercy. It was probably
because I was too young
to know when to keep
these things to myself.
You, of course, provided
companionship with
diplomatic silence.")*

§§§

BAILEY

Bailey was a beautiful female Huskie just
about my size, with startling gray eyes and a thick
coat of white fur. She lived just down Florida Road
with Ingrid. Ingrid was very proud of Bailey and
kept her groomed and washed so well that Bailey
always looked her best.

In a town the size of Maynard, there weren't any leash laws. Dogs ran free unless their owners wanted to isolate them or make them into guard dogs. Neither Bailey nor I had any restrictions on when and where we went, except that we were both trained to be home by dark. Bailey and I were equally wise about the dangers of the road.

Bailey and I would pal around with the neighborhood children, go sliding on Reed's hill, and splash in the creek that ran across our back yard. We were friendly and got along. She wouldn't go too far from home alone, nor would I, although with Boy I would go anywhere. Bailey would accompany Ingrid anywhere as well.

I have learned that infrequently, female dogs go into heat. What that means is that they are mature dogs ready to mate with a male like me to produce puppies. Female dogs in heat throw off a most tantalizing odor, unbearably attractive to males. I know! We males become a real nuisance to owners of a female. Male dogs for miles around may come flocking to her house, trying to get an opportunity to mate with the female. If she is a purebred dog with AKC papers, the owner will most likely keep her in the house so she would mate only with a selected dog of her own breed.

Well, Bailey came into heat. I knew it. I knew it intensely, as she lived just down the street. By watching me, the LaCroix knew it also, so they tried their best to keep me in the house. I whined.

I scratched on the door. I paced back and forth. and I finally slipped out of the house when Boy came home from school. You know where I went.

About that time, Bailey gave her owner the slip also. We met down by the creek at dusk that evening and did what nature had prepared us to do. Ingrid was able to catch up with Bailey then and there, so she knew that it was I, Blackface, with whom Bailey had connected.

I'm a mongrel as you know, although my parentage was very purposefully selected. My potential fatherhood was something of a disaster to Ingrid's folks. But inasmuch as I had demonstrated how gentle and amiable a dog I was, and was of comparable size to Bailey, they began to accept the idea of my siring a litter of Bailey's pups. They began to guess what features each of us would bring forth in our offspring.

Well, puppies are puppies, at least for the first two months. When they arrived, one could see different fur colors and patterns right away. There were six of them, evenly split between males and females — blind, cuddly, and mewing. They seemed always to be hungry, and Bailey was a very good mother to these puppies of ours. I cannot say I had anything to do with raising them. I just watched them grow from time to time. When the mewing turned into yips, when the wobbly legs became sturdy, then the six of them would crowd

63

around me and pull on my ears and legs and generally pester me with attention. It was a joy to know these wonderful little fellows were part of me.

Eventually, the puppies were weaned and took on the stature and shape of mature dogs. Their personalities developed, and they established a pecking order among themselves. One of them, the male with the most energy, became top dog or pick-of-the-litter. He was the first to leave. In the span of a few weeks, all our puppies were placed with families with children. It pleased me to know that people trusted my pedigree, assuring themselves that their new pet would turn out to be a good child companion.

I've often wondered where they went, what kind of lives they led, and would I know them were we ever to cross paths again. Would they recognize me? Later on in the city and on jaunts around town, I would scrutinize carefully every dog I came across, wondering, "Is that one of my puppies?" I never got over the curiosity.

§§§

("Blackface, I never told you about the anguish I went through when my

folks said, "No" to my pleas to get one of your puppies. They were such handsome responsive cuddly little fellows, I could hardly bring myself to go home for supper.")

§§§

CHAPTER THREE: FORT POND

IN WHICH I MEET A SKUNK
AND WIDEN MY CIRCLE OF FRIENDS

St. George's Camp

Summer in Maynard meant going to Fort Pond. Boy's father and mother were determined to find a way to keep the young people in their church busy during the Depression. Large numbers of people were unemployed. Few had any money. There were no ready jobs for teenagers. So the LaCroix started a camp. From nothing.

They scrounged beds, sheets, chairs, pots and pans. They convinced a Littleton dairy farmer to rent two shacks he owned on Fort Pond, which the St. George's parishioners fixed up enough to do the job. There were no windows — only screens to keep the bugs out. I liked to go inside in the heat of the day to get free of the flies as well as get in out of the sun. As you remember, I've got a big fur coat that goes with being both collie and Saint Bernard.

The LaCroix also scrounged rowboats and

canoes, and even got a church boarding school to give them an old pairs-and-coxswain shell that needed fixing. I never went out in that tippy thing, but I loved to be taken for a ride in one of the flat-bottomed rowboats.

Boy was just right to be cox in the shell. He sat in the back looking where the shell was going. He did the steering with ropes that operated the rudder. His mother and father rowed with their backs to the front, only able to see where they had been. I wouldn't like that at all. Every time I go riding in the car, I want to see what's in front of me, head on the side of the rumble seat, nose out over the fender, smelling the breeze. Riding backwards is like living in the past.

§§§

> *("Look who's talking about living in the past. All the things you've talked about so far are re-creating your past life. Which is not so bad, really. It's like returning to a restaurant where you had a great meal.")*

§§§

THE ACTONS

I loved to go to Fort Pond, riding in the rumble seat, thinking ahead and anticipating the joy of freely romping all over the campgrounds. We would go through South Acton where the cider press threw off such great smells, and West Acton where Boy used to go to kindergarten. We'd stop for groceries at Tracy's General Store, where Mr. Tracy's daughter Geraldine was always ready to slip me something good to eat.

From West Acton, the narrow road went through farmland, with the smell in the air of new-turned earth in the spring and hay in late summer. The road paralleled the railroad, and on the way back, we'd often drive right alongside the local train taking milk, mail, and passengers into Boston.

I felt as though we were in a race, scooting along beside this big noisy machine. It clattered along, playing rhythmic patterns as the wheels crossed the regularly-spaced rail joints. It sounded like the standard snare drum pattern:

'Paradiddle-paradiddle-paradiddle'........
When the train crossed a switch,
it changed to: 'Rad-a-ma-cue'........

The train ran beneath a cloud of smoke that had that distinct odor all coal-burning steam engines used to have. You probably never smelled that great odor. All the trains now run on oil or electricity instead of coal. You modern kids just miss out on a lot of great smells.

After the railroad tracks branched off to the left, we'd go up a hill to Farmer Buell's apple orchard, which had another great smell: rotten apples. Even in early summer, that odor hung in the air as we drove through the orchard. The ground was still sprinkled with rotting apples left from the previous fall.

Abruptly, the smells changed as we passed through a gap in the stone wall and entered a pasture that sloped down to Fort Pond. It was dog's heaven.

§§§

("Farmer Buell was a dairy farmer and his barn was off limits to you but not to me. I would wander up there at milking time and watch as Mr. Buell would milk the cows by hand. It was before

*automatic milking
machines. I loved to watch
the tabby cats, sitting high
on their haunches,
begging for a squirt of
hot milk in the face. Buell
would empty each full
pail into one of those tall
metal milk cans. When
he had emptied all his
cows' udders. he put all
the cans full of hot milk
in a pool of cooling water.
Every day, a truck came
by and picked up his milk
to take to the pasteurizing
plant. When one is a dairy
farmer, one can't take
a week off or go on a
vacation. The cows have
to be milked each and
every day.")*

§§§

POOP

The hillside field was pockmarked with cow flops. The new ones were moist and acrid, not particularly good to sniff and worse to step in, but there were lots and lots of nice old ripe flops, ones with a crust. These delicacies had been rotting long enough to mellow out, and they produced nature's most elegant perfume.

I speak as a dog, of course. Mrs. LaCroix didn't think much of cow flops, fresh or mature, especially when Titania stepped in one that memorable night. That was the time the girl campers put on their version of Shakespeare's *Midsummer Night's Dream* in the pasture. Mrs. LaCroix was the director and was hard put to make the best of it in the face of the fuss Titania put up. Shakespeare would have loved it.

While we're at it, I might as well talk about privies, out-houses, or as the Colonial Virginians used to call them, "necessaries." There was no indoor plumbing at St. George's Camp. Water came from a hand pump over a dug well and was carried indoors in a bucket for cooking and dish-washing. Functional elimination (fancy words meaning going to the bathroom) was waterless — no flush toilets of the sort you take for granted.

There were two outhouses, each a two-holer, set off from the cabins. You might think they would smell extremely bad, or in the minds of us dogs, delicious. Actually, they were quite mild as odors go, as they were frequently sprinkled heavily with lime, a way to neutralize the acids. Boy had only one complaint, and that was that it was spooky, having to go out to the privy at night with a kerosene lantern to light your way. Of course, I had no use for the privy as I couldn't manage the seat.

§§§

("Puzzle: Cow poop, sheep poop, and horse poop make great fertilizers. Then, why does dog poop kill the grass? Probably because dogs are meat-eaters and process food much more efficiently, so there's a lot less food value left in the residue. You digest food much more efficiently than grazing animals.")

§§§

Girls Camp

At St. George's Camp at Fort Pond, I was the only dog. But I didn't get lonely at all, because the month of July was boys camp and August was girls camp. The first part was neat, rough-housing with the guys. The second month was just as much fun but very different. I got petted and hugged to the point I just had to get away from it under the cabin sometimes. The girls would find my tickle spot — all dogs have a tickle spot you know — and it would turn me into the likes of a purring and contented kitten. I love to have my ears scratched too, and they found just the right spots, with just the right gentle touch only girls have. Ah, girls camp.

I remember as though it were yesterday the time I met my first skunk. Talk about furious women! It was at the girls camp that first summer, and I thought this little fellow was a kind of kitty I'd not come across before. I get along fairly well with cats; they don't bother me. I don't chase after them anymore, after I got scratched pretty bad on my snout by the church mouser. Anyway, here's this black and white kitty in the pasture one evening when I go out to relieve myself. He sort of stamped his feet when I got near but that didn't tell me anything. I got a little closer, not growling or anything. And then this creep turned his back on me and squirted me with the most awful stuff.

I like a good smell, as you know. But this? It stank! I stank! Every girl I got near shrieked and ran away from me. They not only wouldn't let me in the cabin, they drew straws to see which one took me up the hill on a rope and tied me to an apple tree that night. How embarrassing!

Farmer Buell came and took care of me the next day. I could tell he wasn't too pleased to have to come anywhere near me either. Dear friend, never get near one of those kitty-looking creatures, especially if they start stamping their feet. When they turn their back on you and lift their tail, at least close your eyes. The stuff stings as well as stinks!

§§§

("I well remember your escapade with Mr. Skunk! How could anyone forget? It was a major trauma for everyone at camp and not just wretched old you. I ought to mention the reference to your tickle spot, centered and just below your ribs. It's not the same with people. We're tickleish under our armpits.")

74

There was a place across Fort Pond owned
by a friendly couple, "Unc" and "Florence."
Nobody ever called Mrs. Wood "Flo." It just didn't
fit. She was a jolly soul and very bossy, but
everyone liked her 'cause she was so outgoing
and generous. Unc was tall, kindly, reserved, and
let Florence set the pace. Have you ever noticed
how people often have dogs that sort of reflect
themselves? Well, this couple had dogs like that.
Unc's companion was a friend of mine named
Greta, a Great Dane with the gentlest of manner,
a real lady. She had the run of the house and
grounds and I had many a great visit with her. We
got along very well, even though she was a good
foot higher at the shoulder than I am, and I'm
considered a big dog. She sort of loped along when
she walked, in slow motion. Her legs had to move
further on her than they did on me so it all took
longer. And I had to look up every time we got
together. It made my neck sore. I guess kids have
the same problem talking to grown-up people,
always having to have your neck bent back to see
their faces.

Florence's dogs were German Shepherds
and except at night, they spent all their time in a
fenced yard. They were gentle with their mistress
all right, but fierce guard dogs to anyone outside

the family. I drove them batty, trotting around outside their fenced enclosure and teasing them. It's a good thing that fence was strong and high. Florence's Shepherds would have mauled me something awful. They would have made that Chow I had a fight with look like an amateur. I shiver at the thought!

You might have guessed that Florence's dogs would have been Golden Retrievers or Gordon Setters to reflect her sociability, but it turned out to be just the opposite characteristic that her dogs reflected. There's no accounting for people's taste, is there?

§§§

("You ought to be ashamed for taunting those German Shepherds. It was almost as mean-spirited as going to the zoo and throwing rocks at the bears. If you had just gone over to their fence and made nice noises, let them smell you and get used to you, they might well have become good friends.")

Florence had a niece named Jacqueline, the same age as Boy, and she spent a lot of time at her aunt and uncle's place. To keep Jackie occupied, Aunt Florence got her a horse.

If you think taking care of a dog is trouble, let me tell you what you have to do if you have a horse. Dogs are self-cleaning, except for those occasions where the dirt we pick up now and then might rub off inside a house. Like cats, we generally keep ourselves clean. But horses have to be washed and scrubbed and rubbed down and curried and have their hooves scraped and their mane combed out. They have to wear shoes, too, special metal shoes that are nailed on. How would you like it if someone nailed your shoes on in September and you wore them all the time, in the bathtub, on the beach, and even in bed? There would be no tippy-toeing down the stairs on Christmas morning; you would go "clump! clump! clump!" and wake up the neighborhood.

So I'm glad not to be a horse. Especially when you realize they have to cope with a metal stick in their mouth and carry folks around on their back. I don't mind little kids climbing on my back now and then, and horses are of course a lot bigger and stronger than us dogs, but I'm sure horses would just as soon not have to carry big fat people around. It makes them sway-backed, like a clothesline carrying a weeks laundry.

Horses don't make horse flops like cows do, all gooey. They make horse buns, called that I guess as they are sort of shaped like dinner rolls, and pretty neat. They are drier, firm, and don't smell quite as good as a good year-old cow flop, but they smell pretty good when fresh. It was always pleasant hanging around Jackie's stable. That's a delicious combination — hay, oats, and horse buns.

Another great smell that lingers in my memory from Woodscamp is the smell of pine needles and pine sap. The house sat on a rocky point of land covered with tall pines, and the ground was blanketed with a thick layer of long white pine needles. In the summer, the hot needles would throw off such a magnificent resinous smell I just loved to lie down in them, all stretched out. Some of the pine sap would stick to my coat so I could smell of pine for days. I guess Mrs. LaCroix liked to smell pine too, 'cause she didn't demand I get washed right away, like she would if I had rolled in a dead fish or something.

§§§

*("Jackie was the first
pretty girl I ever felt*

*comfortable with. She
made it easy to talk to
and do things together.
Part of it was that I was
always on her turf rather
than on mine. But the rest
of it was that I just plain
liked her.")*

§§§

WATER WORKS

At Woodscamp they had a cook named
Nancy, a magician in the kitchen and a jolly person
who liked dogs nearly as much as she liked people.
Her place was a center of good smells all day long,
an endless variety of tantalizing odors that drew
me to her door like a deer to salt. She was always
good for a nibble if you hung around her kitchen
door. It really drove those German Shepherds
crazy to see Nancy giving a visitor dog a goodie
right in front of their gate. They would bark and
bark until they were hoarse. I loved it, being able
to taunt those fenced-in dogs. Mutts like me love
to give it back to those haughty purebreds when
we get a chance.

Unc and Florence liked Boy as well as me, as he and Jackie served as companions in a world of adults. They would go sailing on the pond, and swim off the dock, and on rainy days play cards indoors on the veranda. I was welcome inside as long as I didn't get wet, but if I got rained on, it was out under the pine trees for me. It's that funny old business of people not liking the smell of wet dogs.

Now, when Boy and Jackie went swimming, I usually joined in. They would jump off the dock with a big splash, which is a way of getting in the water I really dislike. My way is to wade in slowly until I begin to float. Then I swim the way God meant us all to swim; I do the dog-paddle. That's the natural way you first learned to get about in the water. Then they taught you fancy strokes with your arms coming out of the water, and how to hold your breath when your head went underwater. I always keep my nose above water.

When I get out of the water, I have a habit of shaking my body vigorously to get most of the water out of my fur, not being able to handle a towel. It's a game I play: how many people can I spray when I go into my shake? You ought to have seen everybody scurry away when I would come out of the pond. It was great fun running around to each person and trying to spray them. It was a game of 'spray' instead of 'tag'.

§§§

("It looks so easy, Black-
face, when you shake the
water off, but it isn't. I've
tried to shimmy and shake
like you do but all I do
is wriggle. What's your
secret? Still, when you
have to get all dried off to
be allowed in the houses,
for instance, you never
object!")

§§§

MISSING FRIEND

Coming back to Maynard at the end of the
summer, I wandered down the back lot and over
the little bridge to see Bailey again. When I got to
her yard, something just wasn't right. It all smelled
differently. There were cat odors about and

nothing of Bailey's scent. I could see people inside and they were strangers. It dawned on me that Bailey's family must have moved away while we were at Fort Pond. Alas!

There was no possible way I could find out where Bailey went. There was a finality to it as if she had been hit by a car in front of me. I moped around for days, wondering where she might be, what she might be doing, and blaming myself for causing Bailey's folks to move away. I knew I wouldn't forget her. I knew I'd be looking for our puppies for the rest of my life, wherever my path crossed other dogs, I would be forever checking them to see if they were kin to me.

§§§

("That was a real blow, Blackface. I, too, missed Bailey. I also missed her mistress and I have no idea where they moved to. Maybe some day we'll run into one of your pups. They have to be in or around Maynard.")

§§§

CHAPTER FOUR: NANTUCKET

IN WHICH I GET IN BIG TROUBLE

WOODS HOLE

Ministers usually take a vacation in August when many of their parishioners are out-of-town. The expected thing for the LaCroix family in August was for them to go to Nantucket Island. The Diocese of Massachusetts maintained a retreat house in the town. Some thoughtful person left this house for the use of the clergy, who in those days were never paid much and couldn't afford to go to a place where staying in a hotel was necessary.

I would ordinarily be left at home, lonesome and forgotten by everyone save the church sexton. He would come once a day to feed and water me and see that all was well at the church. I hated it when August came around. There was nothing to do except lie out in the yard and pant.

Except for one wonderful summer.

That was the year that the Trustees of Church Haven on Nantucket Island decided to make an exception in my case. They voted to let me come and stay in the small back yard. No dog had ever been permitted at the house before and sadly, as I will explain, none since.

No child had ever been permitted there either, until the Trustees made an exception in Boy's case. He was allowed to come and sleep in the bay window space on the front stair landing, just above the front door. That exception worked out extremely well, and Boy had become something of a mascot to the regulars of Church Haven. It followed that his well-mannered dog might well be allowed on the premises for the month of August.

The day came when the LaCroix's car, now a green Ford sedan, was loaded up with clothing and equipment, gear which included Boy's bicycle tied onto the front of the car, wheels inside the metal bumper. There was barely enough room for me, but I was allowed to sit on the back seat next to an open window. For most of the trip I was content to sit and sniff the different and exotic vapors that came to my curious nose.

We left the rectory in the dark and rode for several hours with the headlights on. The reason for such an early start was to catch the morning steamer out of Woods Hole, and incidentally to have much of the trip in the cool of the day. You should remember that we are talking about a time before cars were air-conditioned.

There was another reason that tickled me no end. We arrived at the pier in Woods Hole over an hour before the steamer left. Mr. LaCroix drove the car up to the steamer, unloaded everything out of the car except Boy's bike. Then he got on the bike and pedaled off!

Why did he do that?

His prearranged plan was to leave the car in the minister's driveway in Falmouth some five miles away and then ride Boy's bike back to the pier, saving the cost of putting the car in a parking lot for a month.

I was allowed on the open decks of the steamer but not inside, so Mrs. LaCroix, Boy, and I sat next to the pier-side rail on the upper deck, waiting and watching for the bike to appear. We waited. All the passengers came aboard. All the cars were stowed on the vehicle deck. All the carts with baggage and provisions were wheeled into the ship. And still no bike.

We could see the captain on the bridge giving orders in preparation for sailing. We watched as the dock crew first slid the big gang-plank for cars back onto the pier. Then the narrow brow for passengers was retrieved and lowered. The stern lines were taken in. Mrs. LaCroix had gotten up out of her chair and was about to rush to the bridge in hopes of getting the sailing delayed.

At that moment, far up the hill leading to the pier, came Mr. LaCroix, pedaling furiously, his knees akimbo on Boy's small bike, his coat tails flying. We could hear the ringing of the bell on the handlebar as he tried to let the ship's crew know he was coming.

The bow lines were being loosened from pier bollards. As those hawsers were being tossed into the water to be hauled onto the ship, Mr. LaCroix came abreast of the brow, and the good-humored dock crew shoved it far enough out that Mr. LaCroix in his clerical collar rode across onto the lower deck of the steamship Naushon, not a moment too soon.

Just then the ship's whistle let loose a long ear-splitting blast that made me cower in fear and pain. But that fear quickly turned to joy when a chorus of delighted cheers arose all around me. Mrs. LaCroix, Boy, and everybody else on the deck who watched the flying bike-riding minister were shouting congratulations. Our exhausted and sweat-soaked man-of-the-cloth finally bounded up the ladder to the upper deck to his waiting family. Everybody embraced and I got patted on the head so much I hid under a deck chair. So began our summer's adventure.

§§§

*("That was one beat-
up bike as I remember,
bought in a repair shop. It
had but one gear, coaster
brakes, balloon tires, and
a hard seat. But it did
have fenders, a luggage
basket, a bell and a light.
And it was mine — except
at Woods Hole.")*

§§§

THE STEAMER

This was my first boat ride on something
bigger than a rowboat. I loved the brisk wind with
its many new odors to sample. I loved watching
the seagulls hover and swoop above the stern.
However, the ship's engine noise was irritating and
loud. The decks vibrated so much I thought the

ship might be alive. The smokestack belched black smoke that smelled oily. Everything on deck had a salt coating which would have been nice to lick, except it was also mixed with diesel oil. Boy arranged for some water for me, I found some shade under a lifeboat, and settled in for an unpleasant sail.

Even though we were blessed with a sunny day and smooth waters, I cannot say I enjoyed the cruise. We passed the "Crossrip" lightship and changed course which made the sun strike the ship at a different angle. To avoid being cooked, I shifted my location under the lifeboat. That was the only event of the crossing and I was happy to hear the clanging of the bellbuoy at the head of the channel leading into Nantucket harbor.

As we closed on the Nantucket pier, the upper deck emptied of people. The ship shuddered alarmingly when it came abreast of the dock when the captain called for reverse engines. There was a great turmoil at the stern as the ship's screws pushed water forward to stop the ship's momentum. The heaving lines were thrown and their weights thumped on the pier. The dock crew brought over the hawsers by hauling in the heaving lines, then looped the hawsers over the iron bollards to bind the ship to the dock. They put the gangplank and brow in place and immediately an impatient surge of passengers began going ashore.

There were lots of people waiting to greet new arrivals and lots of dogs running about. Every time I see another dog, I check them out. They might be one of my puppies. Nothing I saw on the dock looked promising.

§§§

("You were lucky, both going to the island and returning, to have such a calm sea. Had it been rough weather, you would have been seasick and miserable, far more uncomfortable than you were. In rough weather, especially for someone who hasn't got their sea-legs as yet, it's important to stay outside, breathing fresh air free of diesel fumes. Go up to the bow and let the wind keep your air clean.")

§§§

As I stood watching the dogs through the rope rail, a most curious activity then began. A group of men in dark suits and black chauffeur's caps lined up at the foot of the brow and began to sing out the following chant, one after the other, some bass, some tenor:

"Sea Cliff, Sea Cliff Inn"
"Ships Inn"
"Ocean House"
"Gordon Folger"
"Nesbitt Inn"
"Sconset House"
"Wauwinet House"

— and more I can't remember. The chanters went through this chorus a dozen times at least, until nearly all passengers except us had left the ship. We were in no hurry, we had no car to drive off. Eventually, the LaCroix family gathered bags, bicycle, and me together and set foot on Nantucket. I was overjoyed to stand on firm ground with the opportunity to lift my leg on a bollard. I had held it in the whole voyage, not thinking it acceptable behavior to pee on a ship.

Mr. LaCroix hailed a taxi and everyone but Boy piled in for the short trip to Church Haven, a large three-story brick building on Main Street a few houses up from the Pacific Bank. The property went through to Liberty Street, where a small yard surrounded by a board fence was to be my home for a month. While we were inspecting the yard before everyone went in the house, Boy pulled up on his bike, winded from the uphill ride.

I couldn't see out because of the fence but I didn't lack for company. Everybody at Church Haven would stop and pet me on their way in and out and often fed me goodies. There was shelter from rain, shade from the house, birds to enjoy, and the gentle climate of the island in which to bask. Compared to summer in Maynard and Boston, it was heavenly.

§§§

("That crack about being winded wasn't fair. You rode up in a taxi, I pedaled my bike as fast as I could to get there at the same time as you did — and I just about made it. Even Jesse Owens would be winded.")

§§§

Doughnuts

It turned out that I had acquired at least five new masters, vacationers at Church Haven who wanted to take me for walks through the town on leash. I wasn't permitted to run free. Taking me for a walk gave me the exercise I needed and an excuse for them to mosey about with purpose.

I liked to go downhill on Main Street early in the morning. Let's say that Jack and Anne Moses were with me. They would lead me across the cobblestone pavement carefully, pause to let me drench the first monarch elm we came to, and then proceed along the uneven brick sidewalk. Native Nantucketers would be setting up their flower stalls by the granite curb. The freshly-cut blossoms still wet with dew sent out delicious scents, a wonderful way to start a day.

We would wander down to the Pacific Club and peer in the windows at the old men playing an early game of checkers. Beyond the Pacific Club were the wharves, redolent with the penetrating odor of day-old fish. By the time we strolled over to Commercial Wharf where the fishing boats tie up, the boats were all out to sea again but the smell remained. Gulls would be haggling over scraps left from the unloading the night before, and it was my daily pleasure to make them fly up and squawk. They always returned immediately after we sauntered on.

At the Downyflake Donut Shop, I would be tied to the bench outside while the Moses went inside for breakfast. I didn't mind the wait, as the donuts were freshly-made and the odor seeped through the screen door to my eager nostrils. Inside this shop, there were but two features: a counter full of all sorts of wonderful pastries and one wall decoration. This was a big picture of a sad fat man holding a skinny donut next to a smiling thin man holding a fat donut. A caption read:

"As you travel on through life, brother,
Whatever be your goal,
Keep your eye upon the doughnut
And not upon the hole."

Good advice. But in the Downyflake, that was not the choice to be made. All the donuts were made with a center that looked more bellybutton than wagon tire.

On leaving the Downyflake, the Moses and I would swing by the Atheneum. This place, the town's public library, would be Boy's home on those ugly days when a nor'easter would soak Nantucket for two soggy chilly days. He would walk me under his poncho and tie me to a bench on the columned portico while he went inside to read. I would get slightly wet from the spray but I didn't mind. Everyone who went in and out of the library greeted me.

After the Atheneum, the Moses and I would then turn left on Center Street and walk uphill to the Pacific Bank, being particularly careful to avoid the speeding bicycles which would whiz down Liberty and on to Center to avoid the bumpy ride over the Main Street cobblestones. We would turn into Liberty and enter the gate to the back yard of Church Haven.

If it wasn't the Moses, it would be Jamie and Gulli Muller, or jolly chubby Cuthbert Fowler who would take turns walking me around town. The Gray Gull restaurant was immediately across Liberty Street from my yard, so nearly every evening, a crowd of Church Haven folk would come by on their way to dinner. And nearly every night, someone would return after dinner with a goodie they brought from the restaurant. If it wasn't for all those exercise walks I gave my friends, I would have left the island thirty pounds overweight.

§§§

("You didn't know that Jack Moses was an old friend. You never were taken over to Chestnut Hill where Jack was the minister. He and his wife

*were childless and went
out of their way to be nice
to kids. Jack shared my
enthusiasm for trains.
And elephants. He had
pictures and statues of
trains and elephants all
over his study. It was
a great place for me to
visit. It was just my good
fortune years later when I
went to school in
Andover, to find that Jack
Moses had become the
minister there.")*

§§§

BRANT POINT

Boy usually went everywhere on his bike,
which meant that I spent very little time with him.
But one day, he had promised the mother of one of
his friends to bring me around to meet everyone.
So Boy and I took the long walk through town,
past the steamship dock, the Whaling Museum,

past the Yacht Club, the children's' beach, and onto the road to Brant Point. Boy spent much of his time there, as the Gurley family lived in a pre-fabricated house opposite the Coast Guard Station.

In the Gurley family, also headed by an Episcopal minister, were twin boys the same age as Boy: Teddy and Dickie. There was also an older sister, Betsy, who was so pleasant and beautiful that no boy, including Boy, could resist being attracted to her. The twins were very different people. Dickie was an avid sailor. Teddy tinkered with a Model-T Ford. Boy liked to crew for Dickie and I liked his friendly swagger the minute we met.

The first thing we did was to go fishing for sand sharks where the channel comes close to shore. After many false bites and lost baits, Dickie caught one about half my length. The shark flipped and flopped and wiggled as if he had fleas. I must admit to badgering him and barking, to the annoyance of everybody nearby. It wasn't 'til he swatted my nose with his sandpaper tail that I quit my yammering.

After fishing, the boys lifted me up and put me in a dingy, and we rowed out to Dickey's Rainbow, tethered to a buoy. This was a small catboat, one of a fleet of boats with multicolored sails, an island feature. There was just enough room in the cockpit for the three of us. Boy had me lie down so I couldn't see over the coaming or be in the way. I watched as they fastened on the sail, lowered the centerboard, and hoisted the gaff and mainsail. The wind caught the sail and made the boat tip alarmingly, but Dickie let the sail flap loose until Boy could crawl out on the deck and untie the painter that held us to the buoy. Dickie hauled in the sheet, forced the tiller far to one side, and we began to accelerate.

The boat tipped as the sail caught the wind. I slid all the way across the cockpit at the same time Boy and Dickie leaped to the windward rail. The sail flattened and the water behind us began gurgling a pleasant tune. The boat steadied and I could feel the movement through the water even though all I could see were masts whizzing by above the coaming.

We sailed all over the harbor. Every so often, Dickie would say, "Ready about." That was a signal for me to duck, get out of the way, and set my claws as best I could against the coming change. Dickie would push the tiller hard and the boat would start to turn, the sail and boom would come scooting by overhead, the boys would jump across the cockpit to the other rail, and off we'd go in another direction.

I could see why the boys liked it. The wind on my face felt good, the sea breeze smelled good, and I could feel that they both were excited at having control over the wind. But for me it was a bore. I couldn't see over the coaming and was happy to see the sail come down. I leaped into the dingy so fast we shipped water. I drew angry shouts from both boys as we nearly capsized. I couldn't wait to scramble out of the dingy as we came near the shore so I tumbled into the water. I got my fur all soaking wet, and went into my automatic drying-off shake. The resulting spray then soaked Boy and Dickie, which absolutely ruined my reputation with Dickie. Oh, well. I didn't want to go sailing again anyway.

§§§

("I'm surprised at you, Blackface! Petulance doesn't suit you very well. I'll bet if we had asked you to go sailing again, you would have come along! That "I couldn't care less" stuff isn't you at all. We like you especially for your honesty.")

§§§

The Moors

One of the things that the residents of
Church Haven liked to do was to go motoring at
dusk on the moors of Nantucket. Not only was it
cool and quiet but the moors were beautiful in the
fading light. Bare branches of beach plums would
shoot long shadows across the gorse. Birdsong
would follow the touring car. Wildflowers rimmed
the tracks of the sandy rutted roads. There were
dozens of such tracks lacing across a hundred
square miles of the island.

The Moses had brought over on the steamship an ancient touring car with a convertible top.
It had a couple of folding jump seats between front
and back seats and could hold as many as eight
people. With no side above seatback level, everyone could see beautifully, including the view
forward. Jack always drove. He knew the moors
like the streets of his parish and never, as far as
anyone knew, got lost. Of course, he may, as
Daniel Boone was quoted as saying, have not
known where he was, but he never was lost.

I know all this because one evening, Boy
asked if he could bring me along. He thought I
might enjoy seeing the deer. Coming upon a deer
or two was always the highpoint of any moor
excursion. In the early darkness, with the headlights
on, the group would often overtake a deer who,

mesmerized by the lights, would stand still and staring a moment before fleeing into the darkness.

With the admonition to Boy that he was to hold onto me the whole evening, we set out for the moors southwest of Sconset. This was the most remote part of the island and we headed first down the road that led to Tom Nevers Head. An old abandoned resort hotel loomed up on the shore there and served as a landmark. From that point, we headed west into the orange sky of a Nantucket sunset. I sat on the right side with my curious nose stuck outboard, my collar and leash in the grasp of Boy who sat on the jump seat in front of me.

All went smoothly in the beginning. The only mishap was a time we got stuck in deep dry sandy ruts. Everybody got out and pushed the car forward to firmer sand. The passengers were content with enjoying the roll of the moors, the sense of isolation, the distant rumble of the Atlantic surf, and the acrobatics of the swallows out to feed on flying night insects. I could smell the scent of deer in the southwest breeze. Very little conversation went on, and what was said was in whispers so as not to interrupt the mood.

As daylight slid away, Jack switched on the headlights. The lines of the rutted road took on a new importance in the newly-restricted field of vision. One could see just to the top of the nearest rise. As the car came to the gentle crest, a whole new geography opened up. Everyone was on edge in expectation. Would there be a deer in the next swale?

Smack in the middle of the ruts, caught in the headlights, was an animal that truly was astonishing. It was bigger than any dog I'd ever met, nearly as big as a horse, and it was wearing an unbelievable set of horns on his head. My fellow passengers were whispering, "Look! A buck with antlers!" I saw no horns at all nor heard any. I thought a horn was what Jack had in the middle of his steering wheel, something that went

"a—ROO—ga"

I lost my head. In my confusion and overcome with curiosity about this deer, this buck with horns, I jumped out of the car and pulled the leash out of Boy's hand. Off I went in chase of this creature, who bounded off across the moors in great leaps. I followed as best I could but the dense low bushes, which were no problem at all for the buck, made my progress much too slow. Soon, I lost even his scent, ending up in darkness and quiet. Only the distant surf sound and a lone whip-poorwill could I hear. I had run out of earshot of the touring car and out of sight of the headlights in the folds of the sand hills. Unlike Daniel Boone, I was lost.

I pushed on blindly until I came to another rutted road. It was much easier on the feet than the gorse, and starlight made the track visible, so I decided to follow the ruts wherever they led. Now and then, my road would cross another. I would have to make a choice as to which seemed a better option. After a few of these intersections, I thought, "I'll take the more heavily used and harder-surfaced one." I avoided those ruts with deep sand which were harder to walk on. I remembered how Jack had had a hard time driving through soft sandy ruts. In retrospect, those choices were the right ones, if I do say so myself.

Eventually I came out on the pavement of the Siasconset Road near dawn. I was thirsty and tired of walking through sand but I was also afraid of being hit by a car, so stayed off the roadway. I headed west. Something inside me, a sort of inner compass, told me that was the direction we had come from. And so it was.

Very few cars passed in the early light but when the sun came up the traffic increased. One of the cars stopped, a man got out and called to me. I'm a trusting and friendly soul at heart so went over to him. After petting me and looking at my trailing leash, collar and dog tags, he invited me to sit in the front seat of his car. He was particularly thoughtful, rolling down the passenger-side window for me.

In the town of Nantucket, we stopped at the police station. The nice fellow who picked me up took me inside, told the desk sergeant where he had found me, and left. The sergeant found a bowl of water and a donut for me, which I gobbled up greedily. He talked to me gently, looked at my dogtag, and picked up the phone. I wagged my tail, and settled in to see what would happen.

In a very short time, Mr. LaCroix came in the door. He was cordial to the sergeant and thanked him profusely for tracking down my owner. But cordial he was not to me! "Bad dog!" "B-a-a-a-d dog!"

His tone of voice told me everything. I was in big trouble. I was in the doghouse. My head dropped down, my tail, which I usually carry pretty high, brushed the floor. I practically slunk out of the police station behind Mr. LaCroix and tried my best to look small and invisible as we walked back to Church Haven.

Jack Moses and his passengers had spent hours on the moors looking and calling for me. They quit after midnight. So when Mr. LaCroix answered the phone and heard that an Episcopal minister's dog had been found and did it belong to anyone at Church Haven, he had mixed feelings. Happy that I was located, furious that I had caused so much trouble. The greeting I got when people passed me on their way to breakfast was cold. Usually the morning was full of pats on the head and ear scratching, and a joyful "How's Blackface?" Not this morning. It was all stern stares of disapproval.

Boy had slept late, as he hadn't got to bed until one o'clock. Mrs. LaCroix let him sleep, even though I had been returned to Church Haven before nine. So when he came downstairs, full of worries abut his dog and best friend, it was an explosive happiness that enveloped my master.

"Where's Blackface?"

"In the backyard."

"Wow!"

— and out he came flying, leaped on my back, hugged me tight, wrestled me down into the grass, and told me how happy he was that I'd been found.

It's a lot nicer to be told you are liked than to be given the cold shoulder. As I intimated earlier, my transgression cost me and Boy a return invitation to Church Haven for the following year. The Trustees had all they needed of dogs and boys.

§§§

("See? That's the kind of honesty we all expect from you, old boy. That's a great tale to tell on yourself. I'm sorry your escapade got us banned from Nantucket but you're forgiven.")

CHAPTER FIVE: BOSTON
IN WHICH I GET USED TO THE CITY
AND BECOME A HERO

MOVING

In the winter of 1934, my world went to
pieces. Boy's world did the same. It was the year
he was in third grade, he had turned nine in
November and was feeling pretty good about life
in Maynard, the friends he'd made, and the fun of
going to Fort Pond and Nantucket in the summer.
What happened was that Boy's father, the man
with the collar on backward, had accepted a call
to become minister of a church in the Allston
neighborhood of Boston. That meant we all had to
go to the city too — Boy, Mrs. LaCroix, and me.

It was out-and-out devastating! It meant
I had to start all over again meeting new dogs,
establishing territory, learning the short cuts in

the neighborhood, making peace with all the cats, finding out who was a good touch for a handout, which dogs wanted to pick fights, what streets were dangerous to cross — all those essential things one has to learn in order to survive. And worst of all, I would have to wear a collar all the time and be taken out on a leash. In Maynard, I pretty much went where I wanted to and when, with no ropes attached. In the city, it was going to be different.

For Boy, it would be an equally difficult transition. He would have to make a break in the middle of a school year. That meant not only making new friends but having to find his place in the pecking orders that were already established in a new school and a new neighborhood. He had fears: of not being liked, of perhaps getting into a fight, of getting teachers who wouldn't be nice to him, of getting lost in the big city, of being run over by a streetcar — all these worries raced through his head. For both of us, it was a time to stay awake at night wondering what the future would bring, and for me to carry around that smell of worry that people found unpleasant. Nobody would pet me for days on end.

When we actually moved, it was after three hectic days of packing boxes and people forgetting I hadn't been fed or my water bowl filled. It was snowing the morning the van pulled up to take the furniture to Boston.

What happened was that Mr. LaCroix drove Mrs. LaCroix and Boy and a whole back seat full of suitcases into the city and left me behind.

I was frantic! Was I not going too? For a couple of hours, I worried something awful. And you know what dogs smell like when they are worried? Well, I really stunk up the house to the point it was unbearable to humans. Fortunately, Mr. LaCroix returned for me and another load in late afternoon. It hit him in the face immediately, that odor of worry, and he was apologetic and gentle with me as he came and packed up my bedding, water bowl and food dish. He soothed and calmed me down so I wouldn't get sick on the trip to the city.

And so we moved away from Maynard.

§§§

("I wonder if you had some of the same feelings I had on walking into the Boston rectory for the first time. It was very strange. The place had just been re-painted and smelled like it. There was new wallpaper on the walls but

no curtains at the windows and no furniture. There was a sense of possession but also of disbelief: was this really my home?")

§§§

The Rectory

It turned out not to be so bad. The rectory in Allston was on a side street between Commonwealth Avenue and Brighton Avenue. Both avenues had streetcars whose intermittent noises would become a sort of musical accompaniment to life in Allston. The church, parish house, and rectory formed the sides of a quiet courtyard with a comfortable lawn under paw. It wasn't as big as the Maynard yard but it was more than I had anticipated. On the other side of the house was a long fenced yard between the rectory and the blank wall of an apartment house next door. This yard became my yard. I would get let out into this private space without a leash. I could dig there all I wanted to, and there were so many cats using the adjacent alley and so much traffic on the sidewalk that I seldom lacked for something to entertain me.

The Boston rectory was huge compared to the Maynard house. There were three floors and a basement, and I got to choose what part of the basement I wanted to sleep in. It was a lot bigger and better than the back pantry in Maynard, and it had a doorway out to my yard. The LaCroix put up a swing set and built a big sandbox. The big brick wall was good for bouncing balls off of, and Boy would come share my yard after school and on weekends. Passers-by on the sidewalk would come up to the gate and pet me and talk to me.

The church members also wanted to make my acquaintance, which was easy to do, as the church parish hall had a door opening onto my yard. Unlike the situation in Maynard where I was unconfined, in Boston I was always fenced in and ready to be petted. People could count on my being there. I became a habit to many of the church members, a welcome one for me. I came to be quite content with Boston after all.

§§§

("That side yard was a life-saver, not only because you were there to keep me company, but because my father had

*built that huge sandbox
that kept me entertained
for hours. As an only child
I spent a lot of time by
myself and could get com-
pletely engrossed building
roads and bridges and
villages in that sandbox. It
was my education as well
as my entertainment.")*

§§§

EXERCISE

Boy's father arranged for him attend the
Longwood Day School on St. Paul Street in Brookline. It doesn't exist anymore, having been sold to
make way for a brick apartment building, but in
its day it was a very progressive school. It had an
affiliation with the Episcopal church so Boy got to
go there for minimum tuition. Generally, it was too
far to walk from home so Mr. LaCroix would take
Boy and me to school each morning in the car. By
then a Model A Ford without a rumble seat had
replaced the Studebaker. At the corner of Commonwealth Avenue and St. Paul, he would open
the door and let me out on the sidewalk.

Now, every dog seems to have a compulsion to chase cars, and I was no exception. Mr. LaCroix had broken me of the habit early, by tying my collar with a short rope to the rear bumper of the car and driving away slowly enough so I could keep up. Eventually I grew tired of the game and tried to break off, only to find I couldn't. What a frightening shock that was! Every time afterward when I thought about chasing a car, my memory sang out: "Whoa! Remember how scary it can be if you can't pull away and stop?"

So even though I don't chase cars, I love to run alongside the family car at a pace I can handle — that is, if I'm invited. And so it was on St. Paul Street. We would go along together, past the old Dexter School, alongside the park for several blocks, until we got to Longwood Day, where Boy and I would trade places. That way, I got my regular exercise, which kept me in shape to live to a ripe old age of sixteen. That's the equivalent of 112 people years. Regular exercise for a city dog is an essential!

So make sure you too — especially if you're a city dweller like I was — get regular exercise. Take it from me, healthy older folks and dogs like me stay in shape and avoid that couch potato profile. Turn off the TV and get out and exercise. And throw away those potato chips!

§§§

*("You only ran beside the
car on the way to school,
never on the return trip.
That's because most of
the running you did was
along the park that ran
for two blocks north of the
school. Had we let you run
on the return trip, you
would have had to cross
too many streets and we
would have lost you in the
traffic on Commonwealth
Avenue.")*

§§§

NORUMBEGA PARK

I always loved to go to Norumbega. Just
the sound of the name rolling off Boy's tongue got
my tail to wagging. There are a number of phrases
that get a particularly strong response from me

each and every time I hear them. "Naw-rum-BEE-ga" is certainly one of them. Here are a few more:

> "Want to go for a RIDE?"
> "Ready for SUP-per?"
> "Want to EAT?"
> "Time to go to SCHOOL!"
> "Want to go for a WALK?"
> "Go to Fort POND?"
> "Are you HUNG-ry?"
> "Yah! Yah! Yah!"

I confess I never really paid much attention to some other words that should have elicited some action on my part. Other well-disciplined dogs pay attention to: "Sit!" "Heel!" "Roll Over!" and "Down!" The most I will do in the discipline area is "Shake."

Norumbega Park was out at the end of Commonwealth Avenue on the Charles River. The main feature was a big enclosed dance-hall in the middle of the park but that wasn't what I loved. My joy were the amusement rides, the merry-go-round in particular. Boy was permitted to take me on the circular platform if we stayed in the fixed benches. I could never sit up on one of those wooden horses because, as you know, I can't hold on to the pole.

But riding round and round, watching the

world spin by, feeling the breeze on my nose, listening to the mechanical music, and being held tight by Boy was loads of fun for me. Often we would be driven to Norumbega by Mrs. LaCroix, who would wave to us as we came by on the merry-go-round. That would be a signal for me to bark back. It was so exhilarating I never wanted to get off.

Another thing I liked was the "Dodge-em." It wasn't a ride. It was a strange open building with metal floor and metal wire ceiling. The feature was a collection of colorful little cars without any visible wheels. They just sort of scooted around in a fenced enclosure like so many beetles, being driven mostly by boys. I'm puzzled as to what made the cars move. They didn't make the noise a regular car makes nor did they throw out the same odor. Maybe there was an unseen animal inside, being directed by the driver. Whatever was under there had to be pretty stupid — running around full-tilt in the dark without seeing where it was going or what it might bump into. Each car had a stick that went up to a wire ceiling and rubbed against it, producing occasional sparking. Each car had a steering wheel. The driver had a strap holding him in and for good reason. The fun of driving one of these no-wheel cars seems to have been to bump into the other cars — the harder the better! It was fun to watch but you would never get me into one of those things.

Getting bumped from behind is frightening. It didn't matter to the boys. From the shrieks of delight they let loose as they crashed into one another, you'd think they were delirious and out of their minds.

Another thing I loved to do at Norumbega was to chase ducks. I never caught one, mind you, but it's fun to see the ducks change pace so quickly. From an awkward waddle on land, they could leap into the air and fly off, their graceful wings already spread for flight. They could also escape with a wing beat and a fast skid into the river. On a really hot day, I might jump into the water after them, not so much in pursuit but just to cool off — and they were much faster duck-paddling than I could go dog-paddling.

As you know, we dogs can't sweat like you people do. We pant. Our big tongues hang way out of our mouths and drip spittle. As we pant, we pull lots of air over our big tongue and that carries away our excess body heat. It's so inefficient that a river dip is a welcome addition to our own heat-dissipation system. At those times I wish I were either a duck or a person.

Norumbega also had canoes for rent, and I got invited into one of those things now and then. I have mixed feelings about canoes. It's nice to be out on the cool river to watch the ducks and geese. But I don't trust those boats. I'd much rather ride in a row boat with a nice flat floor. Canoes feel tippy, and when I feel the boat is about to roll over, I have been known to stand up and try to jump out of the canoe. That had not been a bad thing to do when just the boys were paddling. They were able to steady the canoe and get me to lie down again. But the day I jumped up and overturned the canoe with Mrs. LaCroix in the bow was the last time I ever got invited to go canoeing.

§§§

("Now, there you go again, that little streak of petulance! I'm sure you got invited to go canoeing with us boys again — but probably never again with my mother along. And you never got invited to go sailing with Dickie and me again on account of your attitude.")

§§§

The Abattoir

There was an attraction in Brighton that most people don't know about. Of course if you lived near it you would know it's there but if you were a person, you would not appreciate it. You would not refer to it at all as an attraction, more likely an abomination. But for us dogs, it's almost heaven. It's the abattoir.

That's a fancy French name for a slaughterhouse, or a place where live cows and pigs and sheep and goats and chickens and turkeys get changed into meat.

I never see the live animals, just the end product. I guess I would find eating meat a terribly hard thing to do if I could actually relate the stuff in the butcher shop to the animals it used to be. But I like meat so much that I've built up a wall in my mind between animals and meat. Some folk call that self-deception or thinking in watertight compartments. I call it common sense. It saves me anguish when I visit.

Every so often, Mr. LaCroix and I go visit the abattoir. I have to stay in the car but Mr. LaCroix rolls down the window for me. I get to smell those butcher-shop smells that so delight us dogs. The aromas of beef and pork, sausage and turkey waft through the screen doors and out to my quivering nostrils. I conjure up in my mind all the special cuts that dogs enjoy but people generally avoid, such as beef heart, calves tongue, pigs feet and ears, liver, brisket, sweet-breads, and all the little poultry delights that come under the title of giblets.

If I'm particularly fortunate, Mr. LaCroix will prevail on the butcher inside to throw in a big bone for me. Such a bone comes out wrapped in waxed brown paper and it always has a respectable amount of meat on it. I can't see it in its wrapper but I can smell it, and I drool all the way home just thinking how much fun it's going to be to gnaw on that bone. Wouldn't you like to chew on a nice raw pigs foot?

§§§

("In a word, "No." I hate to go anywhere near that stinking old slaughter-house!")

§§§

The city had lots of new noises for me to get used to. There was the milk wagon. It came around at dawn, drawn by a horse with rubber shoes, "Clop, clop, clop." It rolled on rubber tires, so there was very little sound except for the clinking together of the glass milk bottles that the driver would leave at houses on his route.

Then there was the rag man. He came around also behind a horse, only his rig made lots of noise — iron horse shoes and iron tires on the cart wheels made a clattering beat to the rag man's loud call:

"Raaaags! Raaaags!"

He would collect worn wool rugs and cloth to be recycled into the braided rugs that were common then.

Another street vendor was the scissors grinder. He would come around with a push cart with a tinkly bell on it. This was the signal to everyone with a dull knife, scissors, hatchet, or rotary lawnmower blade to bring it to this man in the street. He had a big circular honestone mounted on the cart that he could turn with a foot pedal. Between the tinkle of the bell, you could

119

hear the friction of steel against grindstone echoing down the street.

Boston also had icemen, whose pleasures I described when we were talking about life in Maynard. The Boston rectory has both an icebox and a new-fangled refrigerator which was used to keep food fresh. It didn't make ice, so we still put up a card in the window for the iceman.

Most enjoyable to me of all the street merchants was the organ grinder, who would come around with his trained monkey and music box on a stick. The monkey was especially interested in me, another animal to sniff. He wore a little red jacket with gold epaulets on the shoulders, a red fez hat that tied under his chin, a tin cup in his hand, and a light chain around his neck that connected him to the organ grinder. He would go round the circle of people that always gathered and beg for coins. He wasn't sure whether he should be walking on two or four legs, whether he should be a monkey or an imitation person, so he would switch from one mode to the other, depending on whether the organ grinder yanked his chain. I felt sorry for the monkey, who did all the work and got nothing but peanuts in exchange.

The organ grinder with his droopy mustache stood there cranking the handle on the music box and emptying the monkey's cup when it got full. It appeared that he had the easy end of the deal. They didn't come very often but always got a big welcome when they showed up unannounced. It was the same organ grinder every year, but there was a different monkey. Can you guess why?

Would you like to be the monkey-on-a-chain, begging handouts? Getting your chain yanked? I know I wouldn't. It's bad enough having to wear a collar and dogtags around my own neck.

§§§

("I doubt if organ grinders with pet monkeys on a chain would be allowed on the streets today. The Cruelty-to-Animals people would certainly make life miserable for anyone who tried it, even if it was a traditional activity or the city fathers permitted it. At the time, I just thought like you that it was unfair for the monkey to be doing all the work, getting paid peanuts.")

DOG MAIL

I know it's an indelicate subject, but I'm sure you must have wondered about the habit of dogs going around peeing on everything they pass when you take them for a walk. Let me try to explain. Someone told me about seeing a movie about a man who wanted to study wolves in Alaska. He wanted to know how they could survive in the long arctic winters and how they decided which wolf could hunt where. He learned that the wolves were surviving on voles — relatives of field mice — and that there were definite limits to the territory each wolf could hunt on.

Each wolf went around the borders of its territory sprinkling its urine, which had an odor unique to that particular wolf. So the man, in order to establish a precise area he could measure for density of voles, found that if he too peed on all his boundary rocks, he could establish his own hunting ground. And that he did. He could then, by catching his own voles, measure what sort of nourishment a given area of tundra could produce in vole meat. He learned to eat vole stew with gusto.

Because dogs are close cousins to wolves, you can see that what we do when we go on a walk is leave messages for other dogs to read:

"Blackface was here an hour ago."

or

"This particular street is Blackface
Country. Get out."

or

"Let's get acquainted."

We dogs can't read or write, but we have
our own mail system based on urine and smell.
However, one has to have a refined sense of smell
like mine to be able to read the messages.

You may also have observed a dog, after he
has pooped on the grass somewhere, begin scratching the sod vigorously with his hind legs. This too
is a message, sent to other dogs that says, "Here's a
good place to poop."

Bears claw trees to establish territory. Deer
rub their antlers against saplings and also urinate
at the boundaries of their territory. You see, dogs
aren't the only message-writers.

§§§

("I don't know if you ever
observed the way other
dog-walkers react while
their pet was in the
process of pooping. Some
try to appear somewhere

*else. Others try to look
busy. Some are impatient.
Some are visibly
embarrassed. And some
have the decency to pick
up the lumps and take
them home so nobody
steps on them.")*

§§§

HARE AND HOUNDS

I'm reminded, by the talk of leaving
messages around on the streets, of a great game
Boy and his friends used to play, a game they let
me play too. It's called Hare and Hounds. You may
be familiar with it.

One person is chosen to be the Hare. He
or she should be pretty athletic and smart, like a
rabbit, and this Hare is given a piece of chalk and
a ten minute head start. What the 'Hare' does is
this: He leaves a special chalk mark on the sidewalk with an arrow pointing in the direction of any
change he makes, so that the 'Hounds' — the pack
of chasers — can track the Hare.

In our case, we ran this game all over Brookline from Corey Hill to Cottage Farm. The Hare was encouraged to double back and do all sorts of tricky fox-like diversions to slow up the Hounds, for he has that ten minute start and two hours to play. If the pack doesn't catch him in two hours, he wins. By the rules we played by, a frappe (milkshake or malted outside New England) went to the winner. Of course, if he's caught, he buys a frappe for the person who tags him first.

I would get a scoop of frappe in a paper cup if Boy were on the winning side, so I liked to play Hare and Hounds. It isn't often that a St. Bernard gets to be called a hound.

My ability at Hare and Hounds had pluses and minuses. I could follow a scent pretty well if the Hare were going slow and straight, but if he were running and jumping and going along the tops of walls, I'd lose the trail. And of course, I couldn't read the chalk marks at all when it came to knowing where the Hare changed direction. Still, my nose could sometimes succeed where nothing else could, and I had a great time running along with a pack of boys for a couple of hours. As you know, wolves and dogs are pack animals, used to living and hunting in groups, so Hare and Hounds was my just my cup of kibble.

§§§

("It was always great fun when you came along on Hare and Hounds. But sometimes, we got upset when you stopped to check out every dog we came across. I guess you were always on the lookout for one of your puppies.")

§§§

WHAT'S IN A NAME?

It was shortly after we moved to Boston that Boy started to get out from under the name "Boy." The name was used exclusively by his parents and their friends and had been in use for such a long time that it was hard to shake. At Longwood Day School, he was "Eldon" to the faculty and "Eldon"

126

to his fellow students. He had no natural decent nickname and it bothered him. He really wished he had been named "Carson" LaCroix instead of "Eldon," so he could be nick-named "Kit," like the Western pioneer. Anything but "Boy." His father said he had failed to convince his mother of the merits of the Carson name instead of the personal honor of having a namesake. But she didn't want her little boy named after a cowboy.

Boy finally got his parents' friends to stop using "Boy," though it was particularly difficult. He had the same name as his father so that led to a lot of confusion when one of his buddies would come on the phone and ask for Eldon. Was the phone call for the minister or the child? Usually, Mrs. LaCroix could tell by the quality of the voice. I know I could tell, just by overhearing the telephone sound, if it were any of Boy's friends.

"Oops!" There I go, using the name "Boy." Excuse me, friends of Eldon. I just can't get the name "Boy" out of my old shaggy head, so I'm going to keep on using it to describe my master for the rest of this story. Please forgive me.

§§§

("Thanks a lot, old buddy! You KNOW how

I hate that name. I had another name problem too. I got into the habit of calling every male I meet "Sir." It began in the family as the polite way to address people older than I was — porters, taxicab drivers, anyone. Then in those private schools I was sent to, and in the Navy, it was "yes-sir-nosir" all the time with teachers and officers. After the war, it took disciplined concentration on my part to stop the habit.")

§§§

CROQUET

Stephen, Billy, and Art were Boy's closest friends at Longwood Day School, all the same age and in the same classes. Stephen lived nearby in Brookline on Dwight Street and could walk to school. Billy lived on the Worcester Turn-pike overlooking the reservoir and had to be driven to school, and Art lived first in Lynn and then in Winchester. He had a very long ride every day. There weren't any dogs at Steve's or Art's but Billy had a couple of Golden Retrievers I could play with when Boy and I would go over there.

Stephen's father made us all welcome at the Dwight Street house, just so long as we kept out of his vegetable garden. I had to be on a leash to go through his garden; it was placed between the street and the place the boys played croquet.

Now, there is a game that drives me crazy. I want to chase the balls and carry them around in my mouth so the boys will try to get them away from me. I was a pretty artful dodger as a young dog and could keep a croquet ball in my mouth a long time before someone wrestled me to the ground and retrieved the ball. And of course it was all nice and sticky with my saliva, which they didn't appreciate at all. I had to learn not to chase the croquet balls or I would get tied up back on the porch. I learned to sit on the sidelines and watch the action, but they did allow me to bark when it got exciting.

And it did get exciting! These kids played a very lively and mean game of croquet. No quarter was given, none at all. Most of the fun was in bashing an opponent's ball to the other end of the lawn. And nothing made one of them happier than when an opponent missed his ball and whammed the mallet against his own foot instead. Howls of pain mingled with howls of delight, and I could join in louder than anyone with my "Bark! Bark! Bark!" It often brought Steve's mother out with a pitcher of lemonade to see what all the commotion was about.

Boy and Stephen were the closest of friends. They lived near each other, they went to school together, they played after school together. But it's strange how even being that close they could get on each other's nerves and come to blows. I never would have believed it if I hadn't been there one afternoon on the Longwood grounds after school.

These boys were playing on one of those contraptions with a swivel on a high metal pole holding four or five dangling ropes. The object was to grab a rope and run clockwise 'til you could become airborne. It would take cooperation for five kids to make it all spin around in unison, with five bodies twisting round the pole and flying in formation.

This day, Boy wanted to go at one speed and Stephen at another. They kept frustrating each other to the point when one of them swung and hit the other. I don't remember who started it. But right there on the cinders, Boy and Stephen squared off and slugged it out, each blaming the other through their tears.

There was no damage done except to their composure, no black eyes or torn clothing. They weren't that good at fighting. It took about a week for them to put aside their hurt feelings and return to a normal friendship. It made my life easier to know there were no lingering resentments that I had to contend with when I went over to Dwight Street with Boy.

§§§

("Did you know what actually broke down our anger with each other? It was when we were forced to cooperate and work together on a school project. It could have been something like making Greek helmets and shin guards for a fifth grade play.")

§§§

In winter, we would go sledding on a hill in a park on Amory Road near Longwood Day School. The boys let me chase them all I wanted to in the snow. Boy and I would come home all covered with little frozen snowballs, as we had spent more time falling off the sled than riding on it. The boys would encourage me to jump on the sled as it was sliding down the hill to see if we all could hang on. This got my fur all iced up too. Mrs. LaCroix would close the doors in the back hall to let me thaw out there, before letting me into the rest of the house. Being a Saint Bernard, I liked romping out in the snow, icy fur and all, and had to be coaxed into coming into the house after sledding.

On a visit to Art's house, I got introduced to a frozen pond and the fun you can have on the ice. It's different from snow, where I can run without slipping. But on the ice, in the beginning, there's no traction. My feet went in all directions. However, I learned to take steps slowly and deliberately, lifting my paws up off the ice before moving them forward. Then I could gradually get up speed. Furthermore, you can slide: _____
_____ a mile!

On this pond near Art's house they played a new game to me: hockey. Each kid had a bent stick with which he pushed around a little round black pill called a puck. I thought it would be easy for me to play this game. Being a dog — no opposable thumb on my paws, you know — I wouldn't have to hold anything but could bat the puck around with my paws. The boys thought it great fun to see me slip and slide as I went after the puck. I must have been a funny sight, like a huge ungainly kitten playing with a catnip mouse. I guess I was more clown than hockey player but we all had fun. Now and then it's OK to laugh at oneself.

Another winter activity happened late in the season when the snow was saturated with water and turned into slush. The boys would play in the slush, making dams and sluiceways, ponds and other channels in the slush to redirect the melt water. My delight was to walk all across their construction area making round imprints with my paws and busting gaps in their dams. I could get away with this mischief because none of the boys wanted to tackle me in the slush and come up soaking wet. All they would do is yell at me, "Go Home!"

§§§

("You really ticked us off, running around and messing up our wonderful slush constructions.

133

*It didn't matter that it
would all have to be
redone the next day after
the overnight freeze and
the next day melt. We
suspected you did it to be
funny. Hah!")*

§§§

Loud Noises

There's a picture in the LaCroix photo
album of Boy and me at Logan Airport in Boston.
I'm on a leash, understandably, as nobody wanted
me running around the airport. Until we got close
enough, I thought those winged creatures were
birds I could chase after, like so many Cormorants
drying their wings. The leash was the only thing
that kept me from chasing off after a Stinson
Reliant or a Piper Cub. Those were the days when
light planes could fly in and out of such a big city
airport, before people began flying on commercial
airliners instead of taking the train. Nowadays, it's
no big deal to fly across the country on a big

commercial multi-engine'd jet like the Boeing 747, but when that picture was taken, a Ford Tri-Motor was about the biggest thing in the air.

The Tri-Motor had exactly that — three radial engines with propellers — one on the nose and one on each wing. It was about the same size as today's corporate jet and was covered in corrugated tin. It looked like a shoebox with motors. If you have had the rare luck to fly in a DC-3, a plane that was designed in the Thirties and is still in use, you will recognize the difference between the early planes and today's slick and comfortable airplanes. Nowadays, most planes are moved by jet engines that push back against the air to move a plane forward. A propeller moves a plane by biting into the air and pulling the plane forward — in effect an air screw. The noise is about as bad with one as it is with the other. I'll admit right now I'll keep my distance from all airplanes, either jet or propeller driven. I never want to hear such loud noises again. It is very painful for us dogs to be exposed to such volume. Our ears just aren't built to contend with such noise. We are built to respond to the slightest whisper of a noise, not airplane engines.

And that goes for amplified music too. Please. When you play records or the radio, keep the volume turned down on your loud music. All dogs within earshot will be grateful.

"That leash kept me from fleeing."

§§§

("I think I already talked about playing loud Big Band music. That was on an old record player that had a needle pickup and a primitive sound system. Even that would have given you fits. Amplified music is on another level of torment entirely, not only for dogs but for people. It's frightening to be near this sound and not so much hear the music as feel it vibrate ones bones. It is literally deafening.")

§§§

DOG DAYS

You have probably heard the expression, "dog days." Those are the still hot humid days of

August that affect Washington D.C., especially, and motivate people who live in cities to get away to such places as Rehoboth Beach, Cape Cod, the Smokies, Mackinac Island, Georgian Bay, the Adirondacks, Maine, or Nantucket.

The reason for the phrase "dog days" stems from the problems dogs have with perspiring. We don't sweat through the pores of our skin like you do when you get too hot. All we can do to get rid of excess body heat is to let our tongue hang way out and pant. We cool off through our long tongues, which accounts for the ridiculous way we look in hot weather. It helps also to stay in out of the hot sun as it saves taking in a lot of heat that otherwise would have to be tongue-sweated out. Some dogs like to cool off in water. However, we don't like being sprayed with a hose.

We dogs also have a handicap in that we have to lap up our water. You people have that nifty opposable thumb that allows you to hold a glass up to your lips and pour the water into your mouth. And you also have a smaller mouth. You can pucker up around a straw and suck up liquid. Horses are also blessed with a mouth capable of sucking up water. My mouth can smile from here to Hawaii, but I just can't suck and I can't blow kisses. My style is to lap — to stick my long tongue in water and wipe what sticks to it off inside my mouth before all of it falls off. Cats have the same problem. Drinking beats lapping by a mile. Try

lapping up your Doctor Pepper some afternoon
and see how difficult it is. I can't pucker up and
kiss either. My style is to slobber all over your face.

§§§

*("Blackface, that picture
you describe of a person
trying to lap up a drink is
SO funny! I think I'll ask
my grandson to demon-
strate the process. It ought
to be hilarious — and a
bit messy! And you can
be sure we'll do it when
his mother isn't around.
She'd have a hissy fit for
sure!")*

§§§

On All Fours

It really gets me sometimes to see these
Spitzes and circus Poodles and Chihuahuas walk-

ing around on their hind legs like they were natural bipeds. It's so cute it makes me sick. I can no more balance my body on my hind legs than I can fly. Leave it to the birds to walk on two legs; that's all they've got. Don't you feel awkward sometimes having to walk on only your feet? You know you have perfectly good feet on your arms that you haven't used for walking since you were two years old. All you need is a good pair of shoes for your hands.

You could go everywhere in much more comfort than you do standing up on two legs. You could take away all that stress on your back and stomach muscles that are needed to keep your head and shoulders from falling over. Try going on all fours sometime. It works fine for us dogs and for horses. I ask you, "Who can run faster anyway, people on two legs or horses on four?"

§§§

("You're kidding, of course. Dogs are designed to get around on all fours. People are designed to walk upright. But it wasn't always that way. The evolutionary

predecessors of Man walked both upright and on their front knuckles like a chimpanzee does. Over eons of time, the front legs got longer and the back legs shorter, the feet more compact and the hands capable of fine movement. We lost the need to 'wolf' down a meal. You still eat as if a jackal was about to steal your food away if you didn't gulp it fast.")

§§§

STREETBALL

As Boy got older, he got interested in other people and places and I didn't see much of him except when he would take me along somewhere. He'd come home from school and do his homework or take a piano lesson, or take his bike and ride over to Stephen's house. As we lived in the rectory next to the church, Mr. LaCroix was around the house a lot and would come to pet me rather than Boy.

"Retrieving a home run ball."

Good fellow, Boy's father. Very thoughtful and considerate. Made good stews. I used to listen for his special foot-steps coming up the porch steps and give a mild bark to let him know I heard him come in. We communicated pretty well, we did. After all, he's the one who picked me out from all the other dogs at the Animal Rescue League. As I got older, the relationship became more and more important to me.

But I was still closely tied to Boy. Now and then, Boy would play in Saint Luke's Road with the neighborhood kids, where I could watch what was going on through the gate. They played a city game of baseball that involved the stone steps of the apartments across the street from the rectory. One boy with a tennis ball would be the batter and, standing close to the steps, would hurl the ball hard against the steps, trying to hit the edge of a step at just the right angle. If he did so, the ball would arch high out and over across the street for a home run. The other players would position themselves in the street so as to catch the ball on the fly. One bounce was a single, two bounces was a double. A ball that hit a parked car on the far side of the street was a triple. And over the cars and on my front lawn was a homer.

When someone hit a homer, that was the signal for me to bark long and loud, my way of getting into the game. Someone was always assigned the role of lookout so no one would get hit by a car coming through the street, and there was a regular arrangement for rotation of the players after someone got three outs, much like the usual game of pick-up baseball.

The best part of this game was when someone really hit the step edge just right and the tennis ball would sail over the cars and over the gate into my yard. Then I would pick up the ball in my mouth and dare Boy to take it away from me. I would lead him a merry chase around the yard until I got tired of all the running or he tackled me. I think that sort of football action added to baseball would be great, don't you?

§§§

("Naw. Baseball is fine as is. I wonder if you were aware of nearby Braves Field? Many afternoons and nights in the summer, the curbs of St. Luke's Road would be completely lined with strange cars, making street ball impossible. On a still

night, we could hear the roar of the crowds watching the Boston Braves play baseball under lights. Those Braves moved first to Milwaukee and then to Atlanta and the field is now Boston University's stadium.")

§§§

THE FIRE!

One winter day, as I was lounging in the side yard, lazily watching a squirrel climb the ailanthus saplings when I smelled something different. It was subtle, an odd odor hanging in the air and trying to tell me something. It kept getting more and more potent, until suddenly I recognized it: smoke. Wood smoke.

Boston heated itself in those days with coal, not wood, and St. Luke's was surrounded by apartment houses which didn't have any fireplaces, so wood smoke was unusual. It seemed to be coming from the parish hall next door. And shortly, I could faintly hear the crackle of burning wood, which turned on my alarm.

145

THE CHURCH WAS ON FIRE!

I began to bark as loud and as attention-getting as I could. I really made a commotion, and coming from placid old me, it was startling to Boy's father. He came bounding down the stairs from his study to see what I was barking at. It wasn't until he came around to the side yard that he caught a whiff of smoke and realized that I was telling him that the church was on fire.

He raced for the phone, called the fire department, and flew back across the courtyard with this great big metal hoop he kept the church key on. He wanted to unlock the door for the firemen so they wouldn't have to break the leaded glass windows to get inside and fight the fire.

Loud roaring motors without mufflers! Bells! Sirens! Shouts! My ears hurt just to think of the deafening noise. Men in shiny yellow clothes were running all over the place, pulling long canvas hoses from their red trucks which were now blocking off St. Luke's Road. They broke the windows anyway, even though the door was open. They went up on the steep roof and cut holes to let the smoke and heat out. The flames were visible through the broken windows, and it got so hot next to the parish house that it melted the snow. After two hours, they finally got the fire out, stopped the smoldering, gathered up their hoses and axes, and left.

146

Fortunately, the firemen got enough warning so they were able to get there early enough to keep the fire from burning through the heavy timber trusswork in the parish house and away from the church proper. But there was one very depressed minister left behind. What a mess there was for Boy's father to have to contend with. But you know what he did first? He came over to me and hugged me with tears in his eyes, thankful beyond words for my early warning. We dogs can be useful in ways you might never expect. I felt very proud.

Well, Boy missed all this excitement while it was happening because he was at school. Imagine his reaction when he came home to the tangle of hoses still in the street, the few firemen still staying around in case of a re-ignition, and the disaster visible on the outside of the parish house. He was fearful that more than the church building was damaged or that his parents might have been hurt.

He ran inside the rectory to find out what had happened, to find everyone in the kitchen, sipping coffee and watching the mopping-up operations out in the courtyard. Everyone was all right. I was in the center of the room with a fresh ham bone to gnaw on as thanks for my warning. I got a second hug and a lot of petting from my master, and I think I heard the word hero used several times.

The fire left more than blackened wood and broken windows. It left the unmistakable stink of burning, which lasted for months. I really never got used to it fouling up my nostrils and smelling mechanism, and I could tell that Boy found it unpleasant too. It wasn't until the rebuilding and cleaning operation got well underway that that awful depressing odor disappeared.

§§§

("You know, Blackface, I was never so frightened in my life as I was that afternoon coming home from school. When I turned the corner and saw all the fire engines, and realized that it was either the church or the rectory involved, I literally was stopped in my tracks from fear. But what a relief it was to find everybody in the kitchen alive and unharmed. You are my hero, ol' buddy.")

§§§

CHAPTER SIX: EXPEDITIONS
IN WHICH I GO TO NEW YORK STATE
AND THE STATE OF MAINE

THE TRAIN RIDE

There was the time I took a trip to Cobleskill.

It started out pretty badly for me. At first, I thought that the big box Mr. LaCroix brought home, one with a wire door, might be a new shelter for me in case it rained and no one was home to let me in the house. Mrs. LaCroix and Boy had gone somewhere together so there wasn't the usual reliable help around. I was wrong.

One morning after my walk, Mr. LaCroix put food and water inside the box and induced me to get in to try it out. Then he shut the wire door, latched it, and carried me out to the car. What in blazes was he doing to me?

I was driven to the Allston railroad station and I was unloaded at the Railway Express Office. There, a young friend of Mr. LaCroix took me in hand, and after Boy left, talked to me gently to calm my fears. What was I doing, locked in this box? Was I being abandoned? Did I do something horrible? Why was I here?

Well, Bill did a good job of reassuring me that whatever was going to happen, I was with friends. Bill's father was an engineer on the Boston and Albany Railroad, so Bill had arranged for me and my box to be taken on the train to Cobleskill. Everyone thought it would be nice for me to experience the country, and the train trip would be much easier and shorter than riding in a car.

My box was put in the cab of a big black locomotive. The engineer and fireman were very busy when the train was going through cities and towns but when we got out in the country, the fireman would come over and give me fresh water and talk to me. It was terribly noisy in that open cab, and every time the fireman opened the fire-box door to add more coal, a fierce blast of heat would rock my box. Going through the Berkshire Mountains, the train would slow down and strain to climb the up grades. The sound of the wheels on the track changed to a slow: "click! click! click!" from the "par-a-diddle" sound I had come to know going to Fort Pond.

I must admit to not paying much attention

to all the different odors along the way. My attention was entirely focused on what was going on inside that engine cab. I was still worried sick over my predicament.

On the far side of the Berkshires, we passed through Albany and headed out into the country again, into hills and shadow-filled valleys as the day neared its end. Finally we stopped at the station in Cobleskill. My box was lowered to the ground and I heard a familiar voice.

I had heard Mrs. LaCroix's soprano voice that cut through the train noises. She and Boy had come on ahead in an automobile! No wonder I hadn't seen them for several days. You can imagine my relief at seeing someone I knew, and family at that. Well, not only did I get mental relief but my bladder got relief too as soon as I was let out of that box. A long train ride puts a heavy strain on my otherwise remarkable ability to control my urine flow.

I was quick to recognized Mrs. LaCroix's sister, her nephew Johnnie, and niece Kay. I'd known them from their visits to the Maynard house. I can usually flag a familiar person's identity by odor before I can by sight. Johnnie and Kay were five and seven years older and of course bigger than Boy and less inclined to out-ward expressions of enthusiasm. But their father Francis immediately won me over with his jovial manner and confident voice. I soon forgot the ordeal I'd gone through on the train.

§§§

> (*"It was worth it to have you shipped out to Cobleskill. It was like having a best friend along to share a new adventure. And we shared some dillies, didn't we? Remember when I got stuck in the drainage tunnel underneath Grand Street? Or when I got a fish-hook caught in my ear?"*)

§§§

COUSIN JOHNNY

Cobleskill was home to Mrs. LaCroix's sister Katherine. She was known in the family as "Sister," a moniker nearly as bland as "Boy" but stemming from the fact that she was the Big Sister, the oldest of a family of seven children and the Assistant

Mother. She was also very strong-minded and had as a young woman gone to Washington, D.C., before World War I to study, determined to earn her own living as one of the first American kindergarten teachers. She left Methodism behind, became a Universalist, smoked, danced in public, and established her independence in the grand manner. She married the brother of her Universalist pastor, a scion of an old Upstate New York Dutch family, and settled down to raise her family in Cobleskill. Her husband Francis has a great sense of humor, and gave it a Dutch twist whenever he could. For instance, when he gave people directions for getting to Cobleskill, he followed them with: "It's in Schoharie County, halfway between Schenectady and Schenevus, but a way east of Skaniateles." He gave the names the Dutch pronunciation. You see, he was not only proud of his Dutch heritage but his ability to pronounce all those funny names:

> *sko-**hair**-ee*
> *skuh-**neck**-ta-dee*
> *sku-**knee**-vus*
> *skinny-**at**-a-lus.*

Cousin Johnny took charge of Boy and me right off the bat. He decided that his first responsibility was to give Boy a decent nickname. He chose

"Bud," short for buddy. And Bud it has been between Johnny and Eldon ever since. However, the name didn't stick anywhere else. It helped to know that he had a good name in Cobleskill, and it made the relationship between the two cousins especially close. For Johnny, it was like getting to name a dog. For Boy, it was a new and welcome identity.

Just so Bud wouldn't get any high-falutin' ideas, Johnny assigned him the title of Stooge. If Bud didn't promptly respond with a loud "Yes" to the question, "Are you my stooge?" his wrist would get an "Indian Burn." Such a twist would leave a red mark, which Bud carried around with pride. After all, it was a mark of friendship and affection from his big cousin. Bud's mother didn't approve at all of this Indian Burn business.

Happily for me, there was Oliver (Twist), the van Schaick dog, for me to play with when the boys had other things to do. And there were cats everywhere. Some of them were fair game to chase, but one, Old Mother Cat, sat quietly all day by the kitchen door. She was not to be disturbed. She just looked me in the eye and with great dignity let me know she was not to be messed with. It was clear that she was grand mistress of the premises.

§§§

("I'm glad you brought up that thing about being Johnnie's stooge. I guess I was his stooge in fact as well as name. It was sort of a badge of honor at the time to be called "Stooge." Not only was he five years older but he was at that time two feet taller than I was. I literally and figuratively looked up to him. I still do. He ended up at six-feet-three to my five-foot-ten.")

§§§

THE BEAR

The Cobleskill house on Grand Street had an endless back yard. There was Old Mother Cat. There were chickens to bark at and watch as they scurried as far away from me as their enclosing fence would permit. Rabbits were so commonplace I came to ignore them entirely. There were children to play with next door and a motley group of canines who came and went, none of whom gave me any trouble.

Carr was Johnny's age and lived next door and Cousin Joe lived up the hill. These three loved to play tricks on Boy, the naive cousin from the city. One morning, I saw Johnny leave the house and head for Joe's house with a black fur coat over his arm, strange clothing for July. He returned with Carr and asked Boy if he would like to go bear hunting with them. Boy asked if I could go along for protection, so we all headed up to the woods behind Joe's house.

Johnny and Carr had their BB guns along, and once in the woods, Boy was induced to play Indian scout and lead the group along the chosen path through the woods. Slowly. Quietly. Careful not to step on a twig. Ears tuned to hear a bear. I wondered why Carr and Johnny were looking at each other and smothering snickers.

"RRRRRROARRRRR!"

A big black bear leaped out of the bushes right in front of us! At least Boy and I thought it was a big black bear. We turned tail and scooted out of there, knocking Carr and Johnny into each other as we passed. But instead of following us, those two just stayed put, laughing as hard as they could. And there, with his head sticking out of the bear coat, was Joe, dripping with sweat and also lost in gales of laughter.

I sure felt sheepish, having been gulled so badly. I really should have smelled out Joe in that fur coat. But Boy took it pretty well, after he realized he had been had by the older boys. It became sort of an initiation rite, 'cause after that, Johnny and his friends would let Boy and me tag along on their summer escapades — fishing the Schoharie River, exploring some of the caverns in Schoharie County's limestone hills, and climbing Cobble mountain above Baird's Hollow.

§§§

("You weren't the only one who fell for that 'bear' ruse. I should have 'smelled it out' too, but in a different sense of the word. I'd already seen the coat. But being with the older boys, with guns along, being extra quiet and in a strange woods, I was perfectly set up. I now think back on it as having been a very clever practical joke — on me.")

§§§

I liked Cobleskill. It reminded me of the slower pace of Maynard. There was a busy downtown, with a public park and bandstand. Friday evenings would see everybody at the park to listen to the band concert. There were jaunts to Baird's Hollow to visit Johnny's uncle. The creek running through the valley reminded me of the Assabet River, full of stones that sheltered crawfish, and burbling the same music. There were cows on the next farm to bother, a haybarn to explore, and ducks and geese in the barnyard to look at. I learned not to get close to a goose, as they are touchy and very quick and accurate with their beaks.

There were a lot of new things in Cobleskill to explore. So it was very hard to make that return trip to Boston — in the box, on the train, in the dark, in the noisy commotion of the locomotive cab. Perhaps the unpleasant trip at the end was good for me, in that I felt relieved to be back home, rather than yearning for that wonderful life in Cobleskill. Over time, though, I became victim of a common phenomenon: I began to forget the unpleasant part of the trip and only stored good memories in my brain. After a year I was all eagerness to return to Cobleskill.

§§§

*("Your train rides were
not much worse than
riding in a car in the
Thirties between Boston
and upstate New York.
There were infrequent fill-
ing stations and places to
stop and eat, bumpy nar-
row roads, steep grades,
and poor direction
signs. The cars all had
leaf springs and were
much smaller inside than
today's cars. Everyone was
completely tuckered out
on arrival. We mostly
brought along our own
food and lunched at
roadside tables in the
Berkshires. You, of course,
were fed royally by the
firemen on the trains!")*

§§§

Down East

I felt something was up that spring. Boy would go off with his father into Boston and come back with a big smile on his face and a bag or two in his hands. Mrs. LaCroix would get out her sewing kit and stitch little labels in Boy's new clothes with his name on them. I can tell the smell of new clothes, and I could pick out the odor of cotton sweatshirt and a sweater made of wool — before sweat gives it that nice wet sheep odor. Is that why they call it a sweater?

School ended but it wasn't the usual routine. The green Ford sedan was getting packed with suitcases and readied for a trip. And the nicest thing about the preparations was that I could sense that I was to be taken along. Maybe I'd been forgiven and we were off again to Nantucket.

The day came in the third week of June. The smell of excitement was in the air. Mr. LaCroix came and put a leash on my collar and led me to the back seat where a blanket was spread. My food and water bowls were on the floor. Boy was sitting next to me. Mrs. LaCroix was in the front seat, continually looking around at Boy and me to see if everything was all right.

It turned out that we were off to take Boy to camp in Maine, a full day's journey to the north. Usually I love to ride in the car — on short trips, that is. But this first all day jaunt was too much for me. Even though Mr. LaCroix stopped to let me out about every hour, I got to feeling queasy. All that jiggling and bouncing about in the back got to me and I got sick. I really messed up the blanket about the time we crossed over into New Hampshire. I felt so ashamed.

But instead of getting angry at me, everyone was very sympathetic. They stopped at a small stream near North Hampton so I could drink some cool water and settle down. They rinsed out the blanket so it didn't smell bad anymore. Mr. LaCroix just slowed the Ford down so it didn't jounce so much and he opened the rear window so I could get lots of fresh air.

We stopped several more times, at Ogunquit, Kennebunk, and Biddeford before turning off Route 1 at West Scarboro. The smells came thick and heady once off the main road: chicken farms, goat farms, pine forests with needles six inches thick on the ground. These poured out the most delicious resinous messages. We passed through lots of quaint little Maine villages — North Scarboro, Gorham, West Gorham, then Standish Four Corners, and at dusk we drove through the village of Sebago Lake. At each village, Mr. LaCroix would announce where we were in his best Maine accent:

"Nawth Sca' burra"

"Gur'um"

"Faw' Connas"

161

and so forth.

We traveled another few miles along a winding road with the lake on Boy's side. The black shafts of lakeside trees were silhouetted against the still bright water. I could sense Boy's anxiety and excitement as we drew near our destination. He stopped saying, "Are we there yet?" Ended were the dozens of "alphabet games" played, the songs sung, and the cows, horses, and one-eyed cars counted. This would be his first time spent away from his parents and he wasn't absolutely sure he was going to like it.

In the dark, with the headlights picking it out, the camp sign was a joyous sight. "We're here!" yelled Boy. We pulled in off the road and stopped. I was frantic to be let out and quickly found the necessary tree, dark or not.

§§§

("You found out on the car trip to Maine how much better off you were on the train going to Cobleskill! It may have been noisy and hot but you didn't throw up. Count your blessings!")

Boy and I were joyfully greeted by his friend Art, classmate at Longwood Day School. Art's father was camp director, and after he exchanged greetings with Boy's parents, he took Boy in tow. Duffel-bag and footlocker unloaded, flashlight in hand, we all took the path to the cabin the boys would share with ten others.

This was no temporary tent city. His cabin was a little clapboarded house with shingle roof and windows, tucked in under an umbrella of pine trees. The inside was unfinished, all the studs and rafters were visible, and there were six steel double bunks along the walls. One lightbulb hung in the center, throwing odd linear shadows from the bunkbed frames on the floor and walls. There were but two mattresses. Art and Boy were the first two occupants. Mrs. LaCroix did the honors in adding sheets and blankets to make up his bed for the first time, all the while giving verbal instruction to Boy as to how to do it. Inasmuch as Boy had gone through this routine at the Fort Pond camp, Boy paid his mother scant attention.

I was more interested in the squirrel odors still hanging in the air. Obviously, some critters had wintered over inside this cabin. And I noted that there was no bathroom in the cabin. All the campers in this group of cabins had to walk to a central privy and shower building.

Once Boy was settled in, Mr. LaCroix was barely able to cajole me into getting back into the car. We drove on a bit farther to a small inn on the lake at East Sebago, where I was allowed to sleep out on the veranda. I could hear the waves lapping on the shore. The night sounds of the countryside I could never hear in Boston had a soothing effect. The fresh air and the pine smell, together with weariness from the long trip, put me to sleep so fast I barely felt the hard planks of the veranda.

§§§

("There is something magical about going to sleep to the sound of waves lapping on the shore. It doesn't matter if it's the quiet slap-slap on an inland lake or the crash of ocean waves on a nighttime beach. The effect is the same. Add another ingredient, salt air, and the resultant sleep is instant and sound.")

§§§

"NO DOGS ALLOWED"

We had missed the sign in the dark the
night before but happily for me, we had come a
day early and so the rule was not yet in effect.
I had the run of the camp. I could amble down
to the water's edge for a cool drink and wade
in the crystal-clear water. I could hang around
"Boss" Chalmers' kitchen to smell the goodies she
was readying for the dozens of people who had
come early to open up the camp. I checked out
all the places with interesting smells: the latrines
and bath houses, the leather shop, the infirmary,
the camp store, and the boathouse, my favorite.
There's something about turpentine and varnish,
oakum and caulk, that delights my nose. There
were sailboats and cedar boats, canoes and skiffs,
many needing hull work before launching for the
summer season. There was a crew putting out a
dock that formed a "U" around a central swimming
area. The men were shivering and complaining
about how chilly the water was, but I didn't mind
it at all. There was that Saint Bernard heritage
showing up again, or else it was the heavy fur
coat I wear all the time. The fellows in swimming
trunks who were putting in the dock didn't have
any protection and were all goose bumps.

Boy wouldn't even go wading. He said later that it was mid-July before Sebago Lake water got warm enough to be comfortable. I showed off my ability to tolerate cold by playing "fetch" with anyone who would toss a stick out in the lake. I'd paddle out and retrieve the stick until we all grew tired of the game. It was good to stretch out on the sand afterward in the sun — after I scattered everyone with my body-shake drying off routine. Consternation turned into laughter as I soaked all the men around me.

Art was showing the ropes to Boy and I followed them around for a while. We went through a tunnel under the road to the place where the smallest kids stayed. There I was introduced to a big strutting tom turkey who had the run of the camp. I admit to backing off when my barking got him upset enough to come after me. After all, I didn't have any experience with a bird nearly as big as I was. He made the geese at Baird's Hollow look tame. His tail feathers were fanned, his red wattle was swinging back and forth under his stretched-out neck, and that beak was nasty enough looking that I didn't care to find out if he knew what to do with it. I noticed that the boys gave old tom turkey plenty of room too.

The Junior Unit cabins were being opened after being shuttered up for the winter and had that stuffy smell of mice and dead air. There were crews sweeping out the lead fragments at the rifle range, adding new sawdust to the jumping pits, and stuffing the archery targets with new straw. The clay tennis courts were being rolled and the white cloth line tapes stapled to the ground. The ball field smelled of new-mown hay and the base-paths were being marked with lime.

Someone was in the screened-in chapel in the woods, trying out the organ that had been idle since the fall. Everywhere we went, there was the sight and sound and smell of preparation.

§§§

("I noticed you were checking the other pre-season dogs present like you do every time we're at a place where there are other dogs. I take it none met your expectations? Blackface, if you ever DID run across one of your puppies, what would you do?")

§§§

THE PORCUPINE

After lunch, which for me was a lot of neat leftovers from "Boss" Chalmers, Art, Boy, and I went off to Long Point on a wooded trail along the shore. The day was clear enough so you could see Fry's Leap across five miles of water. No people had come this way as yet this year, so the trail had nothing but animal smells for me to sample. I could sort out the smell of skunk from my Fort Pond experience but the rest of the odors were more subtle. I snuffled up the scent of deer, white-footed mice, squirrel, woodchuck, fox, rabbit, weasel, and snake. I knew all those smells, but there was one strange smell that was very fresh.

We came up behind a slow-moving animal I'd never seen before. It rustled as it waddled along, its coat was coarse and shiny, and it seemed perfectly unafraid of two boys and a big dog. Art knew enough to grab my collar to keep me away from this fellow, a porcupine. I can thank him for protecting me. Surely, I would have been brash enough had I been alone to have gotten my snout stuck full of painful quills. Old Stickleback ambled over to a tree and we watched him climb slowly up about ten feet to the first crotch. I guess he knew who had the better armament.

Art said that one of the camp tests was to be able to swim the mile from Long Point back to the dock. A lifeguard would row a skiff alongside in case you got a cramp or became exhausted. I wonder if I could dog-paddle that far? You see, dogs put out a lot more energy in the water than people. Our paws don't grab much water at each stroke and we try to swim with as much of our head out of water as possible. People have broad palms and can cup their fingers to get more leverage. They can roll over on their backs, float, and get their wind back. But dogs have to keep up a flurry of dog-paddling just to stay afloat at all. So I don't think I ever want to try the Long Point mile test, lifeguard or not.

§§§

("I took that test, Black-face, and barely passed. I was not anywhere near as good a swimmer as Art was. I just didn't have the floatation body for swimming. But as you've noticed, we people can turn over on our backs, float, and get rested. And we can also swim on our backs with much less effort than any of

the belly-down strokes
or your energy-intensive
dog-paddle. You really
have to struggle to keep
your snout above water.")

§§§

SAYING GOODBY

When we got back to the camp, it was twice
as busy as when we had left. The place was alive
with campers and their families, unloading, saying
goodbyes, and exploring the place. My head ached
from being petted and patted by a hundred friendly
boys, but I won't complain. I love to be petted,
have my ears scratched, my rump mussed, and my
back stroked.

We caught up with Mr. and Mrs. LaCroix,
made a final check of Boy's cabin, and said our
goodbyes at the car. Boy was eager to see us go,
no tears, no hugging and kissing except for Mrs.
LaCroix. The anxiety of the previous day was gone
and he felt comfortable.

The green Ford tootled off down the road

towards Boston with me all alone and stretched out in the back seat. I was content to be heading home, though the thought ran through my mind: wouldn't it be great to be a dog spending the summer at Camp.

§§§

("You bet! All the staff dogs at camp were spoiled rotten with attention and food handouts, to the point where their owners were obliged to keep them penned up most of the time. Otherwise, they would have eaten themselves to death by the end of camp. Now, YOU might have thrived in that situation. I've noticed that you may gulp your food but you seem to know when enough is enough!")

CHAPTER SEVEN: SCHOOLS

IN WHICH I FACE LONELINESS,
DANGER AND DIVORCE

HURRICANE

In the fall of 1938, Boy changed schools again. This time, he went to live at the Fessenden School in West Newton, some ten miles from home, and it was as difficult for him to leave home as it was for all of us to move from Maynard. He would again leave behind all the friends at Longwood Day School and have to find a new slot at Fessenden. I would get to see very little of my master from then on, even though he would come home on many weekends.

Mr. LaCroix drove the 1935 green Ford sedan to West Newton on opening day. The car was full of Boy's stuff and me. Boy took me along for the ride and the companionship which he knew and I suspected was going to change. We dogs are sensitive to moods so I knew something was up.

The day was cloudy and blustery, and it started to rain. By the time in early afternoon when we left the house, it was blowing very hard, feeling a lot like the typical northeaster that New Englanders have come to know. By the time we got to Watertown, the wind was rocking the car and the rain was coming in sheets, and by the time we got to Fessenden, leaves were being blown off the trees.

We quickly got Boy settled in his Hyde Hall dormitory and headed for home, as the storm seemed to be getting worse. By the time we got back to the banks of the Charles River by the Perkins Institute, we were blocked by a weeping willow fallen across the road. Mr. LaCroix backed around and retraced his steps to the Watertown bridge and continued on the return trip on Arsenal Street on the other side of the river.

By the time we got into Brighton, the shingles were being blown off the roofs, branches were being snapped off trees, and signs were coming loose from the fronts of stores. I was getting frightened because I could hardly see anything through the windshield and the car was being bounced around enough to make me feel sick. I could feel our tires plow through deeper and deeper puddles, slowing our progress. On Brighton Avenue, power lines were down in front of us, so Mr. LaCroix swung around and came into St. Luke's Road from Commonwealth Avenue going the wrong way for one block.

Thankfully, we made it home but the rain was coming down so hard we got thoroughly soaked just going from the car to the front porch. Ordinarily, I would have stayed outside to dry off but not that day. I got to dry off in the back hall while Mr. and Mrs. LaCroix exchanged experiences.

You see, this was the famous 1938 New England Hurricane we were in and didn't know it. Boy said afterward that he sat on the window seat in the Fessenden library and watched a row of tall Lombardy poplars along the side of the hockey rink fall, one by one, like giant tenpins. The wind blew all the apples off the trees in the school orchard. Afterwards, the schoolboys were assigned the job of picking the good ones up and putting them into bushel baskets for delivery to the Salvation Army.

During the worst of the storm, Mrs. LaCroix had to cope with the worrisome fear that comes from being alone in a time of danger and uncertainty. People can recognize that fear in dogs because, as I said before, we throw off a particular odor when we're anxious. The announcers on the radio she had turned on kept up their descriptions of one disaster after another. Her son and husband and I were out in the storm, so Mrs. LaCroix was far from staying calm and unconcerned.

A shutter blew off and crashed against the side of the church. She stuck towels in the windowsills as the wind-forced rain was coming through the sash frames in torrents. Water was pouring down the chimney into the fireplace and when the gusts came from the east, the whole house shook. As for me, I was just happy to be out of the car and into a nice warm stable house to recover from my queasiness. And I was happy to know that hurricanes come to New England very infrequently.

§§§

("You weren't the only one out in that hurricane, Blackface. Several of my Fessenden classmates were on a train headed for Boston. In Connecticut, on a viaduct along the Long Island Sound shoreline, the tide surge had washed out the tracks. Everybody had to get off and walk back to firm ground in ankle-deep water in ninety mile-per-hour

winds. Miraculously, no
one was washed away.")

§§§

FESSENDEN

Boy and his buddies played a lot of games
that use balls: croquet, football, baseball, basketball, cricket, and street-ball come to mind. Kids
didn't play soccer then as much as they do now
and there weren't any tennis courts around. I
didn't much care for basketball because of the size
of the ball — couldn't get my mouth on it. Baseball was better 'cause the ball is mouth-sized. But
I learned never to try to stop a baseball head-on
after it has been hit by a bat. The ball's so hard it
can jar your teeth loose. I would always make a
dash for the ball from the side so as to lessen the
impact. The same goes for cricket.

Then there's football, my favorite. It has
that funny leather ball with the pointy ends that
takes such crazy bounces. I can usually grab a
football by the end — 'grab' is not the right word.
'Bite' is more like it. What I love is trying to guess
which way the ball will bounce. There's an endless
variety to how a football will fly.

When the fellows are playing touch football,

they let me join in. I block. Well, actually, what I do is get in the way. And the guys love to try to tackle me even without the ball. For a big ole dog I admit to being pretty nimble, and I seldom get wrestled to the ground. I let Boy do it though; that's one of the ways I have to tell him I like him.

One fall Saturday after Boy went off to Fessenden, Mr. LaCroix called to me and asked if I'd like to go for a ride in the car. That's a magic phrase that many a dog loves to hear. Of course I would like to go! Did I ever refuse a ride?

We drove out to Fessenden and parked under the apple trees that had all their fruit blown off. It smelled like farmer Buell's orchard in Littleton. The leash was put on my collar and Mr. LaCroix led me over to a bench alongside a grass field with white lines. There were two groups of boys on the field, one wearing red sweaters, one wearing green. They all had on leather hats with earflaps and chin straps. Their shoulders were oddly big and swollen underneath the sweaters and they had on socks the same color as their sweaters, tucked into high leather boots with bumps on the bottom. I found out that the red socks were Fessenden boys and the green socks were on the Park School guys. You see, from my eye height above ground, the socks are easier for me to use as a way to tell them apart. You probably look at the sweaters.

And there in the middle of the red socks was Boy! That's why we went out there — to see Boy play football. I'm sure you know all about this game so I won't get into the particulars, except to say that Boy played right halfback and was very shifty. He could cut on an off-tackle slant so un-expectedly that the defensive linesmen seldom could stop him. He would pick up five or ten yards at a clip every time he touched the ball. It seemed as though he was either getting nailed by the safety or going all the way for a touchdown.

They played the old single wing formation, with the ball being centered directly to a running back, rather than have the quarterback handle the ball on each snap. All the backs ran the ball and they all passed too — none of this present-day business of the quarterback doing all the passing and not getting his shirt dirty.

I remember one neat play they pulled off, as it went for an easy touchdown and involved Boy. The play started out like an end sweep to the left. All the blockers got out in front of the quarterback, who suddenly came to a skidding stop just short of the sideline with several blockers in front of him. Boy had brush-blocked their left end and then floated out to the right flat. All the Parks defensive players were suckered into going right to tackle the quarterback who, with all the muscle in his 90-pound body, lofted the football across the field. Boy was standing all alone on the opposite side of the field, right in front of Mr. LaCroix and me. Even I could have caught that ball it came down so softly. Boy trotted into the end zone. Touchdown! Pandemonium! Cheers! And barking!

That's the way it went all afternoon. This Fessenden Midget Team (nobody weighed over 100 pounds) ran up 56 points to nothing for Park. It made for a very embarrassing day for Otis, a friend of Boy's who played on the Park Team.

After the game, Otis came over to where Boy and Mr. LaCroix and I were standing and they rehashed the game over cider and cookies. I passed on the cider but got my share of pretty good cookies. It was a great time for tail-wagging, the kind where you throw all you've got into it, so that your rear end jerks back and forth as well as your tail.

That Midget team in the fall of 1938 went on to an undefeated and un-scored-upon year. Fenn, Fay, Rivers, Derby, Middlesex, Park, and Brown and Nichols all got beat. It was little kids against little kids. There were two heavier teams at Fessenden with more prestige, but it's hard to top an un-scored-upon season, even if its players are midgets!

§§§

("I think that was the

high point of my athletic
career. I peaked early!
It was fun, too, more
so when father and dog
could come and watch.
Other teams I played on
afterwards never came
up with the same sense of
camaraderie as those
Fessenden Midgets.")

§§§

UPSTAIRS WAR

The year Boy went off to boarding school
was the loneliest ever for this old dog. It was the
year that Mr. and Mrs. LaCroix were yelling and
fighting upstairs. With Boy out of the house, they
found my presence in the basement unimportant
and lashed out at each other with harsh voices. It
made me very unhappy to have these two people,
who had taken care of me and given me so much
affection, be so angry at each other.

When Boy came home for a weekend there was a truce. Peace reigned and I got to see my master, whose hugs helped me forget the turmoil in the house. Sage, Boy's closest friend at school, would come home with him now and then. That meant I got to climb upstairs and be nice to the company. I could lie in front of the fireplace and get warm and toasty, watch the flames, and listen to the wood cells pop. The boys would take me out for a walk at a far faster pace than Mr. LaCroix's, and they were apt to go a different route than he would. We could often surprise some alley cat as we cut through the backs behind the apartment houses. And the odors of people's cooking made such walks in the early evening particularly sweet to the nose.

The Fessenden year ended. Boy went off to camp again on Lake Sebago in late June, to stay until the last week in August. There was quiet for the most part upstairs, as Mrs. LaCroix spent most of her time taking courses at the university across the Charles River, and Mr. LaCroix pretty much kept to himself. I would see him only when he brought me food and water. Now and then he remembered to take me for a walk.

Boy was back for a few weeks between camp and his new boarding school. It was time spent gathering together the clothes and other stuff he would need there and greeting briefly his old Longwood friends. Mrs. LaCroix was nowhere to be seen or heard. She had left Boston to take a job teaching English in Florida. A sadness not much different from the feeling I had when Natalie died came over me, when I realized that the family I had come to love was breaking apart.

What could I say? What could I do? I felt miserable, seeing these two people who were my friends and intimate companions separate. The screeching confrontations, the stomping on the floor above me, the crash of broken glasses made me want to cover my ears and flee. Boy had yet to realize what was going on. He was off at school and camp when the fighting was hot. I would never know how he took the breakup. He learned about it weeks after he settled in at Andover.

§§§

("And it tore me apart. I bawled and blubbered and thought the world had come to an end. My dorm proctor Norman Vuillameer was an enormous help in returning me to sanity. That whole year was a period of adjustment to

the fact that my parents had split. I felt I had been abandoned and somehow it was my fault — which of course it wasn't. Coming home to you on weekends now and then was important. You offered the only sense of loyalty I felt. It took thirty years for me to come to the conclusion that I had NOT been abandoned, that my father and mother were really great people who were just incompatible.")

§§§

ANDOVER

I was allowed to ride in the car when Boy was driven up to Andover — Mr. LaCroix driving, Boy squeezed in the middle of the front seat straddling the gearshift lever, and me next to the window, cracked so I could sniff the breezes. The back seat and trunk were filled with the things a boy in the ninth grade felt were necessary for a normal life.

Boy was soon to be fourteen and we would have known each other for nine years. The trip was comfortable, even though we were cramped. It felt great to be riding with Boy's arm around me, the good smells of the road floating across my nostrils, and the sight and sound of the traffic adding excitement to the trip. It just doesn't get much better than that for a dog.

At Andover, Boy was assigned to live in a huge rambling white clapboard dormitory that looked a bit like a summer hotel. A collie named Bessie lived there with her master the house-master, and we made quick friends. It was a most unusual thing for Mr. LaCroix to do but he unleashed me, seeing there was such an easy bond between the Stott dog and me.

The car got unpacked and the gear hauled up three flights of stairs to the top floor. Near the time to leave, I was given the unusual privilege of going up to see Boy's room. It seemed as though each one of those 45 steps was higher than the one before and I was panting when we got to the room. It was nothing to get excited about — just single beds, dressers, wood desks and straight chairs for two people. Boy had a new roommate.

The only thing curious about the place was a long coil of hemp rope under the window. It was explained that the rope was the main escape route in case of fire. You were supposed to throw one end out the window and shinny down fireman-style to the ground. That didn't solve the exit problem for us dogs at all. I couldn't wait to get out of that building.

After saying goodbye to Boy and Bessie, we drove around the campus a bit. It was immense compared to Longwood Day School, huge compared to Fessenden. Elm trees formed green arches over formal pathways. Vast lawns linked brick Colonial buildings, which framed a vista centered on a building with a tall clocktower. I began to feel envious of the dogs I could see on campus, with all this space to investigate and all those trees to mark. And I did my usual check of all those dogs I ran into, looking for my puppies.

I got to make my particular mark on an elm growing beside the tall bell tower, just as it was banging out the quarter hour in descending tones. All clocks with bells sing the same song, played out in four verses. I can hear that clock song in my head today. When I hear those tones in that particular sequence, I always see that Andover bell tower in my mind's eye.

Like many old dogs, I got pretty deaf in my old age. And when you're hard of hearing, some-

185

times you feel sound through vibrations, even though you can't actually hear the notes. It's a different phenomenon from hearing a memory. With bronze bells, especially the great big ones with the low, low tones, even people with good hearing like you can feel the vibrations in the air. When I went deaf, vibrations were what I heard.

§§§

("The bells in that tower not only played the hour but in the right hands, they could produce mystical music that would float on the breeze for miles around. Near the top of the tower below the bells, was a room for the organist. There was a strange keyboard with wooden levers. The bell-ringer would have to bang down hard on a lever to play a note. It was very hard work but made for memorable languid music. Even pop

music came out sounding
classical because of the
delay between notes.")

§§§

New Companions

When Mrs. LaCroix left the rectory in Boston, and with Boy away at Andover, things got
pretty quiet with just me and Mr. LaCroix in the
house. I could hear the mice scurrying through
their pathways in the walls. I could hear the
living room pendulum clock ticking upstairs. I
could hear the faint hiss of the leaky toilet on the
second floor. Quiet.

Mr. LaCroix not only missed the noise, he
missed the activity, and he did something about it.
He decided that all those rooms upstairs shouldn't
be going empty either, so he set the house up as a
dormitory for MIT students. In no time at all, the
place was alive with engineers, doctoral candidates,
Dutch, Germans, and Finns, and even a very nice
Mormon from Utah. The Episcopalian minister and
the Mormon became particularly good friends.

What a bonanza of attention that became for lonely old me. I got to spend lots of time in the kitchen, taste-testing for all those scientific types. Food that got forgotten in the refrigerator for a while was my specialty. They shared their oatmeal with me. I got to gnaw on all the meat bones and the leftover scraps. There's always going to be a soft spot in my heart — and stomach — for those MIT men.

They were also a great boon to Mr. LaCroix, who not only got mental and social stimulation from the lively evening talk, but the students were always offering to fix this or do that chore around the house. It made for a great mutual aid society.

§§§

("For me, it was a peculiar event to return to my home and meet for the first time a bunch of new people who felt just as much at home there as I did. I soon began to look forward to coming home to these new 'older brother' friends from MIT — even though I felt something of a stranger in my own

home. After the war, I would bike over to Cambridge and come back in the evening where even you, old buddy, were a part of a different social scene.")

§§§

CHAPTER EIGHT: WAR
IN WHICH I PULL OFF ANOTHER RESCUE
AND MAKE MY DEPARTURE

HOME FRONT

In l941, America entered into World War II. On the Home Front, as non-military life was called, all sorts of new happenings occurred as a result of the war, in particular rationing. I remember that meat was one of the main things that was rationed, as that loss cut pretty close to home for me. Meat, sugar, butter, gasoline, heating oil, rubber tires, and other ordinary staples of life became scarce. One would get a little booklet of stamps from the government and when you went to the grocers, you not only paid money for the goods, you also gave up some rationing stamps. What goods were left after the Army and Navy got what they needed were distributed to civilians according to a priority system of stamps and stickers. Everybody in the country became involved. Kids collected tinfoil. Every community had a Draft Board which selected at random young men for the Army, regardless of standing in the community. To buy War Bonds to pay for the war was universal.

As the country began focusing its effort on defeating Germany, Italy, and Japan, the flow of new civilian cars ended; all the cars I was tempted to chase were oldies. As a clergyman, Mr. LaCroix had a priority sticker on his car permitting him to buy a set number of gallons of gas a week. It wasn't as high as the sticker a doctor would have, as doctors used to make house calls in those days and needed a car to get around. But it wasn't the lowest either. If you had a "D" sticker, you could just about drive around the block. Veterinarians in the city who treated dogs and cats got a "D." But veterinarians in the country where they looked after horses and cows on widely separated farms got "A" stickers.

Mr. LaCroix was too old at 45 to be drafted into the service but wanted to do what he could. He had been a seaman in the Navy in the First World War, having enlisted while a senior in college. In 1942, I used to drive out with him every week to an airport in Beverly where he took flying lessons. He thought he might learn how to be a ferry pilot, someone who flew planes across the Atlantic so the young fighter pilots with quick reactions didn't have to do the trans-Atlantic flying. He soloed in a Stinson, but immediately after that, his instructor got called up into the Army Air Force.

   Mr. LaCroix never got up enough trust in anyone else to continue his flying lessons, so his Log ends at his proud solo. I remember how dejected he was when he returned to the car in Beverly, the day he heard his instructor was leaving. He just sat in the driver's seat staring straight ahead. It was my signal to go over and lick his face to cheer him up. That rough sticky tongue seems to work every time.

§§§

("My father kept his flying lessons to himself until after the war ended. It allowed him to back out without losing face. I think it took a lot of guts to have given it a try. Blackface, we all owe you a great debt, fella, for your sensitivity, to know exactly when we need you.")

§§§

The August of 1942 was one of the happiest times of my life, because Mr. LaCroix and Boy took me with them when they went to work on the Mt. Hermon School Farm as a part of the war effort. The regular farmhands were all off in the service, leaving older men and boys to get in the hay, weed the vegetable garden, milk the cows, and slop the pigs. We lived in one of the dormitories that summer, with many Mt. Hermon students who stayed over the summer to work. I was given the run of the campus, except I had to stay away from the cows. They were too skittish to have even an old dog like me around. Worrying about what I might do affected their milk production.

While Mr. LaCroix pulled weeds in the garden, Boy would be out in the hayfield, raking the dry grass into windrows which a machine gathered up and formed into bales. Then the bales had to be stowed in the barn, a dirty dusty operation which nobody liked, including me. It would make me cough and sneeze when I'd get the hay dust in my nose. After five o'clock, the pace changed. Marty might get out his saxophone, or a bunch of fellows would go over to the school gym to play pick-up basketball. That was Boy's downfall.

One evening he went to the gym barefoot and skidded right out of his paw pad. The thick skin on the ball of his foot completely sheared off, leaving a raw bleeding foot on Boy and an oval callous stuck to the varnished gym floor. Howl? I couldn't have done better. Boy let everybody know within half a mile that his paw hurt like blazes. The nerves quieted down next day but that injury put him on crutches for a week and made him useless for farmwork.

That's when I earned my keep that summer, keeping Boy company while everyone else went off to work.

§§§

("I remember teaching my-self to play the saxophone when laid up with that raw foot. That was the second time I had to use crutches to get around. It wasn't at all like Maynard, when I was short enough for you to be a help. Remember back when I was small enough to ride around on your back?")

§§§

When I was younger and impetuous, always running off to investigate things and sniff at landmarks, nobody wanted to take me to the Public Gardens. I was too much to handle with all the distractions there. Even on a leash I was a problem, as other dogs on leashes would come by and we dogs would rub noses and sniff rear ends as polite dogs do when meeting. This seems to embarrass people somehow. Anyway, I was big and willful enough so that whoever took me had a hard time pulling me away from other dogs.

But in 1942, Mr. LaCroix would take me to the Public Gardens now and then. I was twelve years old. That's like being 70 in people ages, and I had slowed down and mellowed. I didn't need to pay attention anymore to each and every youthful fellow dog that passed. I didn't even feel I had to respond to the heady perfume of a female, the call of the wild in me that was so overpowering back in Maynard.

That didn't mean I couldn't enjoy a walk in the park. In the Boston Public Gardens, there's lots to see. There are the usual wonderful ducks. I never got tired of watching ducks, either on land or on the water. The ones in the Public Gardens are pampered no end. No dog is allowed there unless on a leash, so ducks and pigeons and squirrels go wherever they want without fear of being chased by a dog. Little kids are something else of course. Children don't often have leashes around their necks to keep them from harassing the animals.

The Public Gardens have something that's unique: swans. These are huge white duck-like birds that float around on the pond like so many sailboats. They have long necks and can feed off the bottom without turning tail like a regular duck. I learned the hard way not to get too close to them, having had my black nose tip nearly pinched off. They beat both geese and tom turkeys for touchiness. They have mean dispositions and a very sharp bite. If you cross them, they hiss and come at you surprisingly fast, neck outstretched. So be warned: don't mess around with swans!

The only swans you want to get near are fake. They sit at the rear of the boats that move around the pond and each one is hollow. The driver sits inside the large fake swan and pedals the boat. You wouldn't know that from the side at dog's-eye level. There's a bridge over the middle of the pond so you can look down on the boats as they pass underneath and watch the drivers knees pump up and down as they pedal away furiously.

Swans, ducks, pigeons, and squirrels. I guess if I had to choose, I'd pick squirrels over even ducks. I'm fascinated at the ease with which they scamper up and down a tree-trunk, as if they had magnets on their paws and the trees were made of steel. They never trip or slip. I've never yet seen one fall out of a tree. They can inch out on a thin twig that bends under their weight and use it as a platform from which to launch themselves five feet through the air to another tree — ten body-lengths. Were a person able to do that, it would be a leap of 60 feet! And then the squirrel manages the landing on another narrow twig. It's absolutely amazing! It makes the acrobats at the circus look like beginners. I could watch the circus performances of squirrels all day.

The Public Gardens are a great place to watch squirrels. Not only are there lots of them — they're used to having people around who feed them. The Public Garden trees are big with broad spreading tops, a perfect environment for these tree-dwelling rodents. When squirrels are on the ground begging for peanuts, it's a long run to the nearest safe tree, so you get a great view of how these animals move on the ground. With long bushy tail following, a squirrel makes a series of undulating flowing leaps so that if you squint, the blurred movement looks like a waving rope or a smooth-running sine curve. Squirrels move with both quickness and grace, which is more than I can say for myself.

Compared to squirrels, pigeons are really clumsy except when they take to the air. On the ground, they walk with an awkward jerky motion, with their head bobbing back and forth at every step. They are forever foraging, looking for specks of things to eat in their path and pecking to check if such bits are edible. If someone sits on a bench and opens a bag of popcorn, pigeons immediately sense that their lunch wagon has come. One bird may discover the popcorn source and magically, without any audible signal being given, dozens more birds fly over to get in on the action. The Public Garden birds are fat and fluffy and for good reason. They eat handouts continually all day.

So strolling through the park at a slow pace and watching all the inhabitants was a nice new occupation for Mr. LaCroix and me. He looked at the people, I looked at the animals and wished I were five years younger, when I would have chased the crowds of feeding pigeons to make them explode into the air. I'd also check out all the dogs I met for that familiar smell that would signal, "Here's a puppy of mine."

As it was, I enjoyed stretching my muscles, absorbing the warm sun on my back, and observing the scene in placid contentment. Except for one incident.

§§§

("And that was...?")

§§§

The Rescue

Mr. LaCroix and I were strolling on the path that goes beneath the bridge when I was jerked into alertness. The little girl just in front of us lurched away from her mother and fell into the water. It was obvious she was too young to be able to swim. I reacted immediately, my Saint Bernard genes took over, I yanked my leash out of my master's hand and leaped in to save her. I dog-paddled over to the girl, grabbed her collar with my mouth, kept her head above water, and headed back to the shore. The little girl was shrieking in fear, not only from her abrupt dipping but from being tugged along by a furry animal like me. Her mother reached over and picked up this sodden child when we got within arms reach. I let go when I felt the upward tug and clambered up on the path. Of course, you know what happened then. I shook.

I do it without thinking. I got everyone within ten feet of me wet: Mr. LaCroix, the mother, the girl who was already soaked, and the dozen people who gathered to see what the commotion was all about. One second a hero, the next a goat, I thought.

Well, not exactly. This time, people just laughed at my automatic drying-off shake. The mother hugged me, wet fur and all. The little girl petted my head very tentatively as she was still half afraid. Mr. LaCroix praised me and told everybody that I was half Saint Bernard, and everyone around began clapping. That little girl took her cue from the crowd. She overcame her uncertainty and fear, ran over to me and hugged me tight around the neck. What else could I do but lick her face!

On the way out of the Public Gardens, we passed a vendor selling ice cream bars. Mr. LaCroix broke his rule never to feed me junk food and bought me an ice cream sandwich which I gobbled up right on the spot. I've been on the lookout ever since for chances to rescue little girls in distress.

§§§

("Gee whilikers! I wish I'd been there to see you in action, Blackface. You seem to have a knack for being at the right place at the right time. You know instinctively what to do. You are so cool under pressure. Bully for you!")

§§§

Navy V-12

Boy would go back and forth to Andover on the train instead of in a car. And in 1943, in June, he graduated. Two weeks later he was in the U.S. Navy.

He didn't have to go far as he was assigned to the Navy V-12 Unit across the Charles River in Cambridge. That was a joyous time for me, as Boy got to come home at least part of many weekends. It was in sharp contrast to the months without any sight of him nor any of the petting and attention that we dogs crave.

I guess you have noticed it yourself with dogs you know. We dogs will always greet a friend with tails wagging, a big grin, and if it's permitted, our paws up on your body. Then we might roll over for a little tickle-spot work or stick our snout between your legs as a hint to scratch behind our ears. In times of great excitement, yips and barking are to be expected from us as an expression of joy.

My bark, by 1943, had gotten out of tune from disuse. I'd spent too much time by myself, so that my vocal cords were producing poor scratchy echoes of my former full deep voice. Like Sinatra in his old age, I couldn't hit the high notes full and clear anymore. But like Sinatra, that didn't keep me from exercising my right to sing whenever the occasion called for it. Visits from the sailor Boy were such events.

§§§

("I must admit that it was painful to come visit you in your old age when your body was giving out. Poor hearing, sight barely there, rheumatism in the joints, gray muzzle, and sore footpads all giving you problems. It didn't seem to change your level of enthusiasm though. I still got licked.")

§§§

CONCORD BRIDGE

There was a weekend in the fall when Boy came home, and Mr. LaCroix suggested that, with a couple of the students, we drive out to Concord to see the place where the American farmers fought the British. It's a regular stop on Mr. LaCroix's list of places to show tourists in New England.

So ignoring the drain on his gas ration card, Mr. LaCroix took two students, Boy, and me out to Concord. We parked in the gravel lot and walked — me on leash — across the road to the long path leading to the Bridge. It was flanked by rude stone walls, and covered over with a flaming canopy of fall foliage. Leaves were underfoot and made swishing sounds as the men walked along.

We came to a bronze statue of a minute-man, stiff and alert, with muzzle-loader at the ready. There was the famous Longfellow poem about the "...rude bridge that arched the flood." Beyond was the bridge, an ordinary span now made of reinforced concrete. The original wood one had long-since rotted away.

And on the bridge was a dog, a dog my size who had somewhat the same coloring, and on a leash. So I began tugging on my own leash, pulling Boy along with the vigor that comes from eager-ness. For I sensed something familiar about this dog. And no wonder!

This was one of my...

PUPPIES!

There was no mistaking the body smell that blended those of Bailey and me. Nose to nose we greeted each other. He knew I was a friendly relative right away. We did everything but jump off the bridge in our eagerness to know everything we could about each other, tying our leashes into knots and forcing our owners both to let go. We stood close together, tails wagging so fast they were furry blurs.

Boy spoke laughingly to the other dog's owner, about this tangle of dogdom that seemed to him both odd and wonderful. He'd never seen me quiver like that. And he remarked on how similar we two dogs were.

"Where do you live? Where did this dog come from?"

It seems she lived in Acton and had bought this dog in Maynard for her now-grown daughter.

"Where in Maynard?" asked Mr. LaCroix, who now had joined the group.

"From a Swedish family who lived off Florida Road."

That cinched it. This new friend, Barnum, was one of my pups, now some nine years old. I had finally caught up with my destiny.

They got us untangled. There was no need for a leash on either one of us. We were both quite content to rub noses and romp together in the bliss of finding another creature like oneself.

The effort finally took its toll on my old body and I flopped down on the grass, exhausted.

The Acton lady leashed Barnum, said her good-byes, and off they went, he with his neck turned as if to say, "I really don't want to go."

I barely made it back to the car. We all piled in and I slept all the way back to Boston.

Completely content.

§§§

*("That chance meeting
was wonderful to witness,
Blackface. Did you
notice that your puppy
had Bailey's gray eyes?")*

§§§

Sea Duty — DE 769

Eventually, Boy departed the V-12 Unit.
I remember his anguish and that of Mr. LaCroix
when they knew that Boy had blown his opportunity to continue in the training program for naval
officers. I overheard them talking about it. Mr.
LaCroix used that comforting voice he uses on me
when he sees I'm anxious, and Boy was using that
tone of voice he uses when he feels sorry. Seems
he went at age 17 from an insulating boarding

school life into a situation where the new freedom was more than he was ready to contend with. He said he hardly ever studied for four terms before it caught up with him. All those hours learning three-cushion billiards and other frivolous activities ultimately proved to be costly. Boy was one sad critter the night before he packed his seabag and shoved off for boot camp. His depression transferred to me as well, for I knew instinctively that we would see very little of each other from then on.

He was sent to Great Lakes Naval Training Center and to Quartermaster School in Gulfport. He was assigned to a destroyer escort in the Atlantic, and Mr. LaCroix would read aloud Boy's letters as if I understood them.

He wrote about being so aware of the depth charges on the deck directly over his bunk that he didn't sleep the first night aboard the USS Neal A. Scott. The first night at sea, blacked out (no running lights showing), they ran into a storm off the Jersey coast. It tossed the ship around enough to make Boy very seasick. He un-dogged the leeward hatch on the pilot house and threw up into the night. To his horror, the gale blew the material back onto the signalmen huddled behind the pilot house.

§§§

*("That was the absolute
worst way to introduce
oneself to a veteran crew.
It was several weeks before
any signalmen would even
talk to me, months before I
felt I'd been accepted.")*

§§§

SHORE LEAVE

Boy's ship stayed in the Atlantic after the
war with Germany ended, which was nice for me,
as he got leave to come home twice before I died
in 1945. He would show up at Saint Luke's Road
dog-tired, as the saying goes, from sitting on a
seabag in the aisle of a mail train all night and half
the day on his way home from Mayport or
Charleston.

I wouldn't know anything was up until I felt his footsteps coming down the basement stairs. I could tell it was Boy. I could distinguish his step from any other. I was nearly completely deaf in 1945, but my sense of touch was still working and vibrations trigger that sense. I could still see some, but my ability to focus had deteriorated.

It didn't matter. When he came close, I could smell his scent and knew for certain that my master had come home. He would stoop down and wrap his arms around my neck, scratch my ears, and run his hand down my spine, and I would wag my rump and lick his face and it would be like old times again.

I could still talk, and that is when the last of this story was transcribed with the certain knowledge that my end was near.

Farewell, Boy.

§§§

("And it is my sad duty to report that Blackface died in his sleep at the ripe old age of sixteen.")

§§§

IN RETROSPECT

CHANGES

I now look back and say, "All told, that was a pretty good stay on Earth." Let me run down for you some of the major things that happened on my watch:

❋ The airplane went from a weird canvas-covered contraption used to thrill people at county fairs to a major form of transportation.

❋ Trains went from coal-fired steam engines puffing dense clouds of smoke and blowing steam whistles to smokeless diesels with air horns.

❋ Cars didn't change form that much on the outside, but automatic transmissions were introduced.

❋ The roads that automobiles ran on changed from two-lane dirt to four-lane concrete divided highways with limited access.

209

❋ The rag man, the organ grinder, the knife sharpener, the milk wagon and the ice man no longer can be seen or heard.

❋ The big super-market supplanted all the little owner-operated small shops, the refrigerator became a household necessity, and the vacuum cleaner arrived.

❋ To stay cool in the summer, people replaced their hand-held and mechanical fans with air conditioning.

❋ The Southern states revived their economies not on the backs of slaves but on the back of electric motors and air-conditioning, powered by current from the new hydro-electric dams of the TVA.

❋ Coal was abandoned in favor of oil and natural gas as the fuel used to heat buildings. The coal shovel gave way to the automatic thermostat.

❋ Swimming suits went from knee-to-neck wool to just enough cotton to cover one's Modesty.

❋ War went from mule-drawn artillery to the development of nuclear bombs, from sharpshooters with squirrel rifles and trench warfare to amphibious assaults with air cover.

✸ Telephones started with a box with a crank to ring up a central Switchboard over a party line to a world-wide automatic dial system.

✸ Airplanes went from propeller-driven biplanes that flew at 50 mph to jet-propelled experimental craft that broke the sound barrier.

✸ Radar, Loran navigation, infrared night vision, world- wide instant radio communication, nylon, sulfa drugs, and .... the end of the Nazi Germany.

§§§

("Come to think of, it, old buddy, your life coincided with FDR's presidency. Those were extraordinary times for you, for me, for the country and the world.")

§§§

Whisperings

That's not the end of it, my friend.
Don't weep for old Blackface.
Don't waste any tears over that
furry carcass left behind,
the one you could touch with
your fingers.
You see, now I touch
the minds and hearts of
the people who knew me in another way.
If you meet up with a dog
who asks to be scratched
and licks your hand,
just remember
that Blackface might be there,
whispering in that dog's ear,
saying in
international dog language,
"Fear not, Fido.
This person is a friend."

* * * * * * *

POSTLUDE

*You may have wondered as you were reading
my little memoir as to how I, a dog without a larynx
or flexible lips, could talk.*

*In the first several years as Boy's companion,
I was, as explained early on, mute except for*

WOOF!

*I could, like the Poodle Charlie in **Travels
with Charlie**, communicate in a limited way
(Charlie had a bent tooth which allowed him to go
"fsst" when wishing to go out). We both could receive
messages, although Charlie had the ability to know
what Mr. Steinbeck was thinking as he was thinking.
That's a skill that I cannot claim to have mastered.*

*Anyway, over the years living with Boy, I
learned to control those natural sounds — yips,
whines, barks, growls, yelps, and wheezes into an
intelligible speech that Boy came to understand. I
used my throat and the back of my tongue to modify
sounds into words. Long words like "intelligible"
had to be spoken in several bursts.*

"Blackface"

— About the Editor —

Eason Cross, Jr., FAIA

A Harvard-trained Architect who lives in Fairfax County, Virginia, Mr. Cross has written articles for architectural publications and a weekly column for a local newspaper. He holds several patents as well as many design awards. His interests range from architecture and art to resurrecting Purysburg, SC, and the USS Slater, local and national politics, and watching with pride his children and grand-children flourish.

ISBN 1425163637

9 781425 163631